NO ONE
NOTICED
THE CAT

Frenery handed the completed parchment to the prince, while he held wax to the candle. The prince took off his heavy signet ring and affixed his seal to the wax.

Niffy had finished her ablutions, and now she peered over at the document.

"Oh, do be careful, Niffy," Frenery said, about to brush the cat aside. "The ink's not quite dry."

"She won't smear it," Jamas said indulgently and turned the letter slightly to the right so that the cat could "read" it. "What do you think, Niffy? Have I struck the right note?"

She gave a soft sort of noise deep in her throat and then, leaping gracefully off the desk, proceeded to curl up in the sun on the window seat.

"Now that it's approved," Jamas said, grinning at Frenery, "I'll sign it."

NO ONE NOTICED THE CAT

Anne McCaffrey

WILDSIDE PRESS

NO ONE NOTICED THE CAT

Published by
Wildside Press, LLC
www.wildsidepress.com

Printed in Canada

To Amelia Michael Johnson
my middle granddaughter
who can read this for her own self

W hen Mangan Tighe, regent to Prince Jamas the Fifth, died, no one noticed the cat in their grief for the passing of this good and learned man. That he was of great age and had enjoyed his wits to the very end only served to heighten the sense of loss. Even Prince Jamas wept, though he had often railed at Regent Mangan's firm but kindly control.

"He never allows me any latitude," Jamas would complain to his equerries.

As they all knew that such restraints also kept Jamas from breaking his neck, head, and back (not to mention all tradition), they merely looked sympathetic. Jamas came from a long line of willful, impetuous, gallant, adventurous princes. Which was why he had been orphaned at an early age when his hey-go-mad young parents killed themselves in a carriage race. The entire country breathed a sigh of relief when Mangan, the former prince's counselor, was made regent.

Prince Jamas would have been slightly more annoyed than grief-stricken if he had been aware that Mangan had known to the second when his soul would leave his body. To protect the principality Mangan had made so peacefully prosperous, the wise man had made certain unusual arrangements well in advance of his expectable demise.

One of them had been to surround the young prince, who now had only a year to go before his majority, with discreet advisors. Mangan had also hand-picked and trained all the primary members of the Court of Esphania for their experience and varied skills so that the prince's council would support their ruler and deftly handle any problems that might arise.

But Mangan had never whispered a hint to his prince that his allotted span was coming to an end. Which to Mangan was not sad but joyous.

When the moment arrived, Mangan knew in his heart that he had done as well as he could to preserve Prince Jamas, the prince's throne, and the commonwealth of Esphania. And he smiled as he died.

"Look, he's smiling," the prince said, brushing tears from his eyes, for he had a generous heart and was sincerely devoted to his regent-guardian. "Death must not be so bad after all."

So not even he noticed the cat who slipped with sinuous quiet away from the fold of the bed curtains where she had been maintaining her own vigil.

T hough not even Frenery knew it, the smoky-colored Niffy was one of Mangan Tighe's last and best safeguards. Her installation had been as smooth and natural as many of Mangan's other precautions. In fact, no one was quite sure where Mangan obtained her mother, a beautifully marked silver tiger-cat: not a useless lap creature but a fine huntress with great long whiskers and almond-shaped green eyes, large ears for listening, long legs for running, and thick fur for withstanding the chill of the castle's stone corridors and floors.

But one morning she was installed by Mangan in his private quarters, and he spent a great deal of time with her on his lap, caressing her, delighting in the softness of her thick dense fur, and listening to the even rhythm of her rumbling purr. But, most of all, laying the groundwork for his ultimate precaution. From his throat issued a sort of purr, too, which the cat obviously responded to by increasing her own rumble.

From time to time, she would tilt her triangular face up to him, slowly closing her eyes and smiling as only a cat can smile. The tip of her magnificently plumed tail might twitch once or twice before she pulled it about her feet again and relaxed under his stroking hand.

Miranda, for that was her name, produced three kittens: two black and one not quite black, for the underfur was softly gray and tortoise-shell in design.

"I'd've thought you'd pick a black one," Prince Jamas said when he inspected the litter in Mangan's tower.

"No, no," Mangan said with a little laugh, "this is the one who chose me."

The kit crawled up to his still broad shoulder—for Mangan had once been a redoubtable swordsman— making the regent wince as its claws pierced through the fabric of his overvest to flesh. It settled itself neatly as if it held this position by right. Since it rode there whenever Mangan left his tower, everyone became accustomed to this behavior.

When the kittens were weaned, Miranda took the other two down to the stables, where they became the scourge of vermin and sought no further advancement in their lot. The grooms, being a somewhat superstitious lot, made sure the palace dogs did not bother Master Mangan's cats: not that even the most stupid of the canines would have had sufficient courage to attack Miranda.

Niffy, for that was what the regent had nicknamed the one who had chosen him, lapped milk and ate the tender victuals which the cook daily provided for her on the regent's breakfast tray. She also went everywhere with Mangan. Considerately, his valet put extra padding on the shoulders of his clothing to reinforce the much-clawed fabric.

"That one has barbs on the ends of 'er prickers," the valet said, nodding wisely. "Clings to him like to life itself."

While the regent attended to the many duties of his position, Niffy would nap in whatever sunlight came through the windows of his tower, or—which amused Prince Jamas immensely, for the young man often visited his mentor—sit on the current documents that passed across the regent's desk. As if able to read, she would watch the pen as it scratched across parchment, inscribing letters to notables or documents of state.

"Does she read your final drafts, Mangan?" the prince

asked once when he noticed that her eyes followed the regent's busy right hand.

Mangan chuckled, reaching up to stroke Niffy, who rose under his hand in appreciation, her purr audible.

"No, my Prince, I trust I do not yet need such assistance," he replied, "but she is a very wise one, indeed."

"Wise? A cat?"

"Truly, my Prince. A cat has the wisdom to remain independent of humans and is always able to provide for itself, whereas dogs are dependent on constant care, A cat allows a human to be a friend if we have proved worthy of such an accolade. Yet it is faithful and recognizes that there are times when we poor humans are in need of the companionship only a cat can provide. Indeed, when I am vexed by a problem, I will often ask her to sit on my lap. I have found that stroking her fur and listening to her soft reassurance, I am able to find a solution to my problems."

"The cat solves your problems?"

"No, my Prince," and Mangan chuckled indulgently, "she provides the serenity in which to solve them."

"May I pet her?" the prince asked, lifting his hand toward Niffy.

"Ask her," Mangan replied.

"After all, I am her prince. She'd better permit." The prince was half-joking.

Niffy raised the green almond-shaped eyes she had inherited from her mother and eyed the prince and his hand.

Abruptly, the prince hesitated and then asked in a tone of some deference, "Will you permit me such familiarity, Lady Niffy?"

Niffy tilted her head slightly, as coquettish as any court

beauty, a soft purr audible.

"She permits?" Jamas asked Mangan, to be sure. Oddly enough, he did not wish to lessen himself in his regent's eyes by being rebuffed by his cat.

"Oh, indeed. That purr so informs you," Mangan said and watched as his prince gently, but in quite the most satisfactory manner, stroked the animal.

"I say, she has the most magnificent fur," the prince said, rather pleased by the tactile contact. "I can see why it might be soothing just to stroke her."

"She's a very comfortable person, my Prince."

"Yes, I do believe she is a person," Jamas said, laughing slightly with embarrassment, for he had not really considered felines "persons" before now. In fact, he hadn't much considered the domestic animals in his castle, especially when they provided the services he had come to expect of each, and certainly not as personalities. Niffy changed his perceptions. Dogs he had in plenty, but they helped him hunt.

"Oh, very much a fur personage, my Prince, and more loyal than you might imagine a cat can be."

That incident, when Jamas tried to place it, happened a good two years before the regent's death.

Somehow or other, the prince, though eager to assume total control of his destiny on reaching the age of twenty-one, had always imagined that Mangan would still be in his tower quarters, with Niffy keeping him company, ready to take over vexatious or tedious problems and solve them in his wise, smooth, and clever way. As ruler, Jamas would then be able to do what he wanted to.

"Why did he have to die now?" Jamas asked his favorite equerry, a baron not many years his senior but of a more cautious nature: one of Mangan's most felicitous appointments for Jamas. "I mean, we have that border dispute . . ."

"Ah, but Jamie," and Grenejon Klanto, Baron Illify, slipped into the familiar mode since they were alone in the prince's quarters in that hour after Mangan's death, "you said you knew how to manage that yourself."

Jamas, his mouth open to refute that allegation, closed it. One of Mangan's maxims echoed in his head: *There is no harm to admit error. To compound it with falsehood is most unwise!*

"Well, not as Mangy would have . . . no, he's dead. I can't be disrespectful when he isn't even cold, can I?" Jamas said in a rueful tone. Then he ran both hands through the crisp blond curls that delighted women and irritated him. Straight hair did not sweat as much under a helmet. "No, mine would have been a more direct approach."

Jamas sighed because he was a very able swordsman and had studied classic battle strategy and troop deployment with more enthusiasm than he had coped with the hazards of grammar and spelling. He had, of course, had the very best possible martial training available—as did every male of his line—and had become extremely proficient in every way possible of rendering an opponent helpless, if not dead.

Jamas *liked* fighting. Mangan had studiously avoided martial confrontations. Which, Jamas had felt, deprived his princely self of a chance to show off his prowess, proving his valor and reminding foes that he would be a dangerous adversary.

War is the last resort and the most expensive one, was another of Mangan's maxims. *Diplomacy might take longer but has more lasting results for the commonweal.*

"Not now," the prince went on, "when the princedom is in mourning."

"Not too much mourning, your highness," said Frenery, who had been Mangan's secretary for decades. He bobbed in an effort to show his respect to his sovereign. "The regent did not wish to, ahem, bore the court or put the treasury to unnecessary expense for obsequies which, he said," and Frenery gave a little cough for the regent's idiosyncrasies, "he would not be able to enjoy or control."

Prince Jamas frowned at the plump Frenery. "What?"

"Well, sire, to be sure, you remarked yourself that our dearly departed *smiled* as he passed from his mortal coil?"

"Hmm, yes, I did. So?"

"The regent requested that post mortem ceremonies be limited to a fine meal and good wines with perhaps a libation to his memory? If you were so disposed?"

"Humph," was the prince's surprised rejoinder. He was somewhat relieved that he wouldn't have to endure long-winded eulogies, the longest of which would surely come from Frenery, who was so punctilious about protocol, respect, and stuff like that. Despite his deep affection and respect for Regent Mangan, Jamas had not been looking forward to such rituals. For a man of Mangan's rank and prestige, speakers could waffle on for hours, and he could think of other things that he would rather do on a fine spring day.

"Eat, drink and be merry, huh," Grenejon said with the hint of a smile. "Yes, Mangan would prefer that, sire. He was never one for pomp and ceremony." Grenejon cast a meaningful glance at Frenery, inviting his support.

"Oh, yes, Baron Illify, quite right. In fact, the regent set aside a fine red wine which he hoped could be used for the occasion."

"Did he?" the prince was cheered. Mangan's taste in wines was known well beyond the borders of Esphania: and rightly.

"Yes, bins 78, 79, 80, and 81," Frenery said, consulting the thick sheaf he always carried about with him for note-taking. Several sheets broke loose and fell to the floor, as they often did from Frenery's overfull notebook. Baron Grenejon almost automatically bent to retrieve them.

"Mangan was always forethoughtful, wasn't he," the prince added and then gave orders for a sumptuous banquet to follow immediately after the interment of the regent Mangan's mortal remains.

Mastering their grief, the palace chefs managed a feast of gastronomic excellence.

"Mind you," the head chef said with both honest sorrow and happy anticipation of showing off his talents, "lately the regent hasn't been able to enjoy the rich and highly seasoned dishes of which I am a master. But I do believe I managed to cater quite inventively, titillating his palate without upsetting his digestion."

The second chef nodded, which was all that was required of him when his superior launched on this sort of talk.

"Therefore, we shall contrive to present all the foods I'm sure the regent would have *liked* to have eaten were he enjoying the superb health our prince does."

And he did so, and the prince found that he could put aside his grief quite easily when confronted with pickled neats' tongues, tiny spiced sausages, chilled shellfish, livers cooked with apples and oranges, cold fruit cream soups, and the swan/goose/duck/chicken/ guineafowl/squab entree, and the baron of beef, the racks of lamb and the stunning array of vegetables and legumes which generally accompany such courses. The removes were equally sumptuous: fish, scallops, prawns, lobsters, and mussels simmered in butter and garlic, and the special sauces for which the head chef was renowned.

In Mangan's cellar, a white wine had been set aside for the fish courses, as dry as one could be had, as well as the fine red. Of both there had been sufficient to keep full the glasses of the guests: the principal earls, dukes, counts, viscounts, and their families, all of whom wished to honor the regent. For in truth, Mangan Tighe had managed not to quarrel with any of them, and they all wished to be present to honor his memory. Especially as there was such a splendid feast.

But, first, the prince did his duty by his mentor and guardian. He rose to his feet before the assembled, who hastily rose to theirs. He lifted high his glass, as did they.

"Let us tonight remember, as he would have wished us to, the fine qualities, great wisdom and kindness of the late Mangan Tighe, regent, friend, and mentor. We shall miss him greatly, but we wish him well in the afterlife to which he has gone. May he still be smiling!"

The prince nearly spilled his wine before he could get the glass to his mouth because he felt *something* rub his silk stockinged legs. If the toast he drank was no more than a sip, and if he sat down abruptly, pushing aside the fine linen tablecloth to peer under the table, he was the prince and everyone was just as glad the toast had been so brief.

"What's the matter, my Prince?" Grenejon asked, leaning across his table companion.

"Ah, nothing, nothing," the prince said, unwilling to admit that he thought the regent's cat had just stroked his legs. He brushed the notion aside and applied himself to the superb food.

However, later, as the harpers went from incidental dinner music to the more enjoyable ballad singing, he felt something settle against his right foot. Inconspicuously dropping his napkin, he had a good look under the tablecloth as he retrieved the napery.

Niffy's bright eyes glinted at him in the gloom. Prince

Jamas also noted how many ladies' slippers were standing empty under the long head table.

A touch on his shoulder and he straightened up. A fresh napkin was dangled at him.

"Nonsense, this is fine," he said, waving off the servitor.

From time to time thereafter, he dropped the odd morsel. Each time he felt the weight shift from his foot for a moment or two. When Niffy resumed her position, she purred her thanks. She particularly liked the liver and purred so loudly that Jamas was certain everyone else could hear her.

No matter, his offerings were acceptable to Niffy. After all, Jamas thought, she would be missing her master, so why shouldn't she share in the feast?

Niffy also decided to share the prince's bed, for she was there when Jamas finally sought it.

"Did we feast and wine Mangan properly, Niffy cat?" he asked her, and she gave him her green-eyed smile from her seat on his pillow. He was oddly reassured to see her there. She'd been so close to the old regent she might have taken it into her head to dwindle away. Some animals did when their masters died.

He'd never permitted dogs in his bedroom—not after the first occasion. They were such restless sleepers, always chasing something that got away in their dreams and yipping as well as scrabbling their nails on the bare wood floors. They also tended to smell. Cats, however, were notoriously clean and neat and slept quietly, curled up in mounds of fur.

As he climbed into his bed and pulled the curtains against the draughts that could not be excluded from the castle, he was glad that he had always insisted— from the time he was eight—that he was old enough to sleep by himself and without the ceremonies generally besetting a ruler at bedtime. He had been pleased that Mangan had supported this alteration in custom. His valets and equerries could fuss over him all they wanted in his dressing rooms, but his bedroom was his private place: a fact he appreciated even more after the onset of puberty.

Jamas was as well favored as his ancestors had been, and not just in looks. And he was as lusty as the best, if not as insatiable as some. (Mangan had handled that aspect of his education deftly.)

There just happened to be a secret passage from the West Tower up to the prince's bedchamber. In fact, the castle was rather well equipped with such discreet amenities. Mangan had taught his young charge where every single one of them went and how to open the hidden locks.

"Did Mangan teach you all the secret ways, too, Niffy?" Jamas asked the cat as he pulled his covers up. "Is that how you got here before I could?"

She blinked slowly. He couldn't be sure if that meant agreement.

"I didn't see you on the steps and you certainly didn't leave the hall before I did. I felt you on my feet all night long. Did you get enough to eat?"

Niffy then smiled her feline smile and, seeing him settled, circled a spot level with his head on the spare pillow and lay down.

"You miss him, don't you?" he said, reaching up to stroke her head.

She purred.

"I will, too."

Her purr deepened. She smiled at him again, then tucked her head down. Shortly after that her purr dwindled into silence.

No one quite noticed when Niffy became a fixture in the prince's vicinity. Perhaps they had been so accustomed to her presence with the regent that it was unremarkable.

"You seem to have been adopted," Baron Grenejon said one morning, when he saw Niffy jump up on the prince's desk as Jamas was rereading the latest demands from his south-western neighbor, the self-styled King Egdril . . . Egdril the Eager, he was often called. This "king" had eagerly annexed a small but well managed valley when its count and his heir had been killed in a boating accident. He had eagerly taken, for his second wife, the clever daughter of a duke farther south, acquiring additional lands. He had eagerly disposed of some rather annoying pirates on the Great Inland Sea as well as their ships, eagerly acquiring their routes for more peaceful trades.

"Adopted by Niffy?" the prince said, reaching out to run a welcoming hand down her luxurious, silky fur. "Yes, well, I guess you could call it that. Found her in my room the night of Mangan's feast. Poor thing misses him, and I don't mind. Sleeps on my pillow."

Grenejon raised dark well-formed eyebrows. "Every night?"

The prince laughed because he suspected Grenejon knew that the pretty brunette dancer from the troupe just then entertaining at the castle had eyed the handsome young prince in the manner which often led to beddings. As indeed it had.

"Mangan raised that cat. She's as discreet as he was."

"Hmmm, yes. You know, Mangan was sort of feline in the way he could maneuver around obstacles and problems."

"Like this one?" Jamas said, slapping the document with some asperity.

"Exactly. Now, what would Mangan say we should do?"

Jamas, who was rather hoping Grenejon would suggest a show of force, exhaled an abrupt breath. He gazed out across the room, catching Niffy scrupulously cleaning her claws.

"I'd show him mine, I think."

"Beg pardon?"

Abruptly certain now of a course of action that could be just as much fun as a battle but less dangerous, Jamas tilted his chair back, balancing himself deftly. "Why, we invite our brother ruler to join us in a hunt. I know there's been a report of barguas in the Fial Valley on our mutual border. King Egdril fancies himself a hunter. Well, barguas make excellent sport. Let us show him how we Esphanians deal with . . . predators."

"Oh, an excellent idea, my Prince."

"Good. Make the arrangements, Grenejon. I shall answer this now. Frenery!" Jamas called, and the secretary peered round the door. "A letter! Oh, Grenejon," he added to his equerry, "this won't take long. Have the courier ready to ride."

Frenery was not quite as elderly as he looked or acted, and he wrote quickly in a fair hand, never faltering as he took the prince's dictation. He also nodded and smiled his approval of the courtly and complimentary phrases in which Jamas couched the invitation to his fellow monarch. (Actually, Esphania was a much larger principality than King Egdril's, even after the recent acquisitions. Traditionally, Esphania's rulers were princes; having had their domains as gifts from an emperor long since dead and an empire long since divided into smaller principalities, princedoms, and provinces which had managed to remain intact.)

Frenery handed the completed parchment to the prince, while he held wax to the candle. The prince took off his heavy signet ring and affixed his seal to the wax.

Niffy had finished her ablutions, and now she peered over at the document.

"Oh, do be careful, Niffy," Frenery said, about to brush the cat aside. "The ink's not quite dry."

"She won't smear it," Jamas said indulgently and turned the letter slightly to the right so that the cat could "read" it. "What do you think, Niffy? Have I struck the right note?"

She gave a soft sort of noise deep in her throat and then, leaping gracefully off the desk, proceeded to curl up in the sun on the window seat.

"Now that it's approved," Jamas said, grinning at Frenery, "I'll sign it."

Frenery regarded his prince with wide-eyed concern and managed a little laugh.

"My Prince will have his little joke."

Jamas regarded his secretary with a bland expression. "And what if it isn't a joke, good old Frenery?"

"Oh?" Frenery shot him a worried glance.

Jamas laughed, pleased at the effect of his remark. "Do take this to the courier and urge him to waste no time in its delivery. I would ask you to join us in the hunt, Frenery, but . . ." He grinned again as Frenery waved his hands in dismay. "I do believe hunting barguas is not your favorite occupation. You can mind Niffy for me during my absence. She misses Mangan, you know."

"Oh, yes, certainly, my Prince. Yes, she does, for I often find her in his quarters."

"So that's where she goes when she's not lounging around mine."

"Should I . . . I mean, well, are you . . . will you need . . . that tower?"

"Am I replacing Mangan? That's impossible. No, leave his quarters as they are. It isn't that the castle lacks other apartments, is it?"

And truly that was so, since the castle was immense. The Esphanian Dynasty had thrived since the end of the Empire, and the castle had long outgrown its original keep and battlements, with wings added here and towers climbing out of corners, while storage facilities went down several levels into the solid rock of the cliff. Five generations ago the dungeons had been converted to house the wines laid down every year from the vineyards.

The village which had once clung merely to the skirts of the rocky heights on which the castle perched had turned into a good sized, prosperous city. It had several market squares, possessed craftsmen of high skill in every profession, and did very good foreign business.

The fertile farmlands and the wide river that led to the not too distant sea were well managed. Products from the orchards, fruit and nut, as well as from the vineyards on the mountain slopes, were prized in many parts of the world. Trade was profitable and, now that King Egdril had executed the coastal pirates, was in a period of expansion.

King Egdril with his customary eagerness replied affirmatively to the prince's invitation, and Frenery, with a select group of chefs, equerries, kennelmen, dogs, and servants went to the proposed site in the Fial Valley to prepare suitable, if temporary, quarters.

Torquedy Vale was chosen without hesitation, for the area had not only a rushing river feeding a large and tranquil lake, but flat meadows for pitching tents and grazing horses as well as sufficient space in the forest glade to invisibly house the necessary small army of servitors such an expedition required for comforting amenities. Foresters were sent out to find barguastrace so that the hunt could narrow its search and provide immediate sport.

Once Prince Jamas learned of the acceptance, he went through the lists of his chief nobles, selecting those to accompany him. Mangan had seen to it that Prince Jamas was sufficiently well acquainted with his subjects that he had no trouble choosing the most appropriate.

"Moxtell of Oria is too blind to be safe on a hunt . . ." Grenejon said as he took over Frenery's duties as secretary during the good man's absence.

"Ah, but he'll bring his three sons and two brothers with him, and they'd give a good account of themselves in a barguas hunt."

As his equerry added their names to the list, Jamas continued to stroke Niffy.

"True," agreed Grenejon dutifully.

"Besides, Moxtell might not see, but Mangan said that had interfered not at all with the old Earl's knowledge of what goes on about him."

"Hmm." Grenejon grinned. "Now, about the younger Fennells . . ."

"Be sure their uncle doesn't think he's included. That man needs a bridle for his tongue, and he's just the sort who'd delight in insulting His Eagerness just to have a bit of sport. Address the invitation to Lady Camilla and tell her that if her brother comes, we'll collect the fine he's been appealing in the courts. Doubled!"

"The one Mangan levied on his lands for his last insult?"

"The very one."

"Mangan taught you well, my Prince." Grenejon looked up, then, because Niffy's purr reached a louder pitch. "Are you taking her?"

"If she'll come," Jamas said, having just decided that she should. Niffy regarded him with her green eyes and smiled.

"How?"

"In my saddlebag, of course. Wouldn't risk her riding on my shoulder."

"Wise, considering the pace you usually ride at. Shouldn't wonder she'll join the hunt."

Niffy smiled again.

When the royal party arrived, fifty strong with a sufficient scattering of grayer heads among the young bloods to suggest that this wasn't a youthful escapade, they found all in order. Just as the dust settled, the honored guest and his entourage appeared from the opposite direction.

Prince Jamas saw that King Egdril's retinue included several fair ladies, mounted astride the fine-limbed horses that were bred on the Mauritian coastal plains. The horses' light brown coats and flaxen manes and tails made them particularly noticeable among the larger bays and blacks which the men of the party rode.

The girls were almost as noteworthy as their steeds. Dressed in hunting gear (although Jamas was not certain that barguas made appropriate prey for women), the three girls were certainly attractive: two brunettes and one stunning redhead whom Jamas immediately took to be as strong-minded and willful as that flamboyant coloration. She wore her mahogany hair in one thick plait down her back, where it dangled just above the cantle. That she sat the cavortings of her mount easily suggested to Jamas that she was going to insist on joining the hunt no matter what wiser heads might say.

Of the two brunettes, who had equally long plaits, one was already playing the coquette with Grenejon. The other merely watched, her eyes darting from one face to another.

A nudge from Baron Illify reminded Jamas that his first obligations were to his fellow ruler.

Jamas kneed his favorite chestnut stallion toward King Egdril and held out his hand.

Egdril was in his middle years, fit and spare of frame, one hand steady on the reins of his fractious mount, which snorted at the proximity of another stallion. The two rulers both nodded as they forced their horses to obey their leg aids and come to a halt side by side. Egdril had very white teeth in a tanned face, a carefully cropped beard that was more white than black, framing a strong face. His eyes took the measure of this young prince, and Jamas returned his forearm clasp with equal strength.

They both laughed at this initial test of each other's worth.

"We meet at last," Egdril said. "And at a splendid site," he added, twisting in his saddle to gaze around him at the tenting and visible accommodations. Servitors were already dashing forward with beakers of thirst-quenching beer.

Accepting his, Egdril took a swig and went on. "Let me make known to you my nieces," and he gestured to the three girls and winked broadly at Jamas.

"By all means, do," Jamas said with as broad a grin.

"The Baroness Salinah!" The redhead tilted her head gracefully, though she held her head high and proudly as she eyed the prince in a very open manner. "My deceased sister's only child. The Ladies Willow and Laurel are my widowed sister's daughters." The names evidently did not please Egdril. "My sons," and he made a broad gesture to bring two riders forward.

"Geroge is the elder and Mavron the cadet," the king said, and both men — older than Jamas and Grenejon and, to judge by the scars on their faces, warriors of some experience — made properly respectful short bows to the prince.

Then Jamas introduced the more important members of his entourage, Moxtell, whose male companions were eyeing the three girls, and the Fennells, whose uncle had seen the wisdom of remaining at home, and went down the rankings to Baron Illify.

"But now, Egdril, dismount and accept my hospitality. Our friends can mingle and get to know each other without more formality."

So they all swung down from their saddles and handed their horses over to the grooms awaiting them.

"He brought fifty, too, if you include the girls," Grenejon said in Jamas' ear.

"I can count."

"Oh, what's that?" cried red-headed Salinah as Niffy emerged from the saddlebag where she had made a comfortable journey and, leaping down, loped off into the nearest copse.

"My cat," Jamas said.

"Your cat?" Salinah's tone was a combination of distaste and contempt.

"Your cat?" The echo came from the lips of the brunette, Laurel, and her voice combined surprise with interest.

"You and your cats, Laurel," Salinah said. "Can't abide the creatures."

"You prefer dogs?" Jamas asked politely enough, but he had lost all other interest in the girl.

"There is a use for them," she said and then turned her head in the direction of the excited barking of the great, shaggy barguas-hunting dogs. "May I?"

"Baron Grenejon will escort you, Baroness Salinah," Jamas said, turning away from the redhead to bend a smile on Laurel and her sister. "As *you* no doubt appreciate, a cat is an individual."

Salinah gave a sniff as Grenejon escorted her away.

"Let me accompany you to your quarters, Egdril," Jamas said, neatly twining the arms of the two girls in his as he led the party. Egdril grinned at the maneuver and fell in step beside Laurel.

Jamas found himself of a height with his fellow ruler, though perhaps not as broad as the more mature man. They could certainly look each other straight in the eye, which subtly reassured the young prince.

It was fortunate that Frenery had thoughtfully provided six private chambers within the arching domed tent of the royal quarters. The king obviously approved as he set foot on the thick carpets that decorated the floor of the entry.

Casting a quick eye about the large interior chamber, Jamas saw that it was comfortable, not ostentatious, though fruits and other dainties had been placed on the tables by the piles of cushions which were traditionally used on such progresses. An appropriately regal wooden chair did stand to one side in case the king preferred it.

Now his retinue began to arrive, setting up the bits and pieces which a well-seasoned traveller like Egdril generally carried in his baggage train, including a much more regal chair. There was a whispered conference as Jamas' steward intercepted Egdril's and exchanged notes. Now men and women arrived with hot and cold finger foods as well as an assortment of beverages.

Egdril sank gracefully onto a pile of cushions, reaching languidly for a hot-house peach.

"Clever, these," he said, patting the cushions with his free hand before taking a bite of the peach. "Not that the ride was arduous but older bones do like a bit of comfort."

Jamas chuckled, denying "old bones" with a flick of his fingers. Willow and Laurel were accepting drinks from the trays and settling themselves quietly.

"Sorry to learn of old Mangan's demise," Egdril added. "Fine statesman. You were lucky to have him as your regent."

"Indeed. He is sorely missed by us all."

With a keen eye, Egdril lobbed the peach pit into a receptacle in the corner and licked his fingers.

"Shall we have good sport in the hunting tomorrow?" Egdril asked and went on before Jamas could assure him so. "The girls are well able to handle themselves on a hunt, even for barguas. I only brought wards who don't faint or act foolish. Salinah's the finest shot with the crossbow in Mauritia. Drives my quarrels right through the middle eye in the target butts."

Just then the two princes, Geroge and Mavron, arrived, accepting wine from the drinks offered as they joined their father and Jamas. Conversation quickly devolved into the hunting available in Mauritia, including the large piscine fighters which offered a struggle to the venturesome. Despite the river Thuler's access to the sea, Esphania was a landlocked principality, so Jamas graciously allowed himself to be regaled with descriptions of the denizens of the deeps and the battles that could be waged between the fisher and the fished.

Shortly thereafter Salinah returned from inspecting his dogpacks. She emphatically informed her uncle that they were fine animals and she looked forward to hunting with them.

"I should like a bath," she said to no one in particular, but Jamas waved toward the private quarters and she went off.

Then Jamas rose to retire and bade everyone a good night. When he entered his own tent, Grenejon was there, looking thoughtful.

"You're expected to choose one of them, you know," he said, pouring the hot spiced drink that Jamas preferred at this time of day. "At least he brought the prettiest of his wards. Seems there have been some most untoward accidents among his nobles, leaving many nubile young women to be suitably married off at Egdril's discretion."

"Not the redhead. I'll leave her for you," Jamas said, peering around the inner room. Then he realized what Grenejon had just said. "Untoward accidents?"

"Hmmm. Well, eight nobles—those who might protest certain measures King Egdril proposes—have unexpectedly passed to their rewards in very recent times. All, seemingly, since Queen Yasmin ascended to her present position. They all left considerable property to the crown. Some say Queen Yasmin disliked them, too. And she's much cleverer than Egdril."

"She did not accompany the king."

"For which we may thank the gods that guard us," Grenejon said fervently.

Jamas grinned. "Then we should be safe enough." He looked about him.

"Oh, Niffy's asleep on your bed," Grenejon said. "So, are you of a mind to enjoy the benefits of matrimony? Forming an alliance that way is much more dependable than any other sort of treaty."

"I know." Jamas made a face, for he hadn't even considered marriage this soon in his life.

"Salinah's too brash anyway, though I think she'll make the biggest play for you."

Jamas snorted. "She dislikes cats."

"You'll have to tell her that, my Prince, for she'd never believe she eliminated herself with the first words out of her lovely mouth. She thinks to win you over with her skills of riding and hunting."

"Did you know that she's able to sink her uncle's quarrels right through the target?"

"That doesn't surprise me at all," Grenejon said and, settling to a cushion, leaned back indolently. He had a smile on his face that Jamas had never seen before.

"Watch yourself. I'm the better prize, and she's the sort will tell you that herself. Besides, that uncle of hers would probably roll up your pretensions and lob them into the nearest bin as he does peach pits."

"If he doesn't, one of those sons of his would," Grenejon said, not the least bit disturbed.

"Gone on her, are you?" Jamas removed his jacket and sank into another pile of cushions.

"As near as makes no never mind."

"Is it safe?"

Grenejon shrugged. "Ah, my Prince, the chase is the thing. Her father was a mere baron, like my good self. And, with all the wards he has to marry off, Egdril might just accept my lands and fine castle. They do march with his border, if only for a few leagues."

"Dream away!"

Afine meal was served in the open, with torches lighting the dining area, their scented smoke driving away the early midges. Spit-roasted meats and baked tubers and vegetables as well as early soft fruit cold soufflés were consumed by sturdy appetites. Though wines were circulated by attentive servitors, the hunters restrained themselves with the view to having a clear head and a keen eye for the morrow's occupation.

The dinner conversation was merry, though Jamas found Salinah a shade too forward for his tastes. Her two cousins said very little, even when he tried to include them. They seemed content to let Salinah dominate. She was, Jamas could not deny, witty, clever, and well-spoken. She took the teasing of her male cousins in good part and gave as good as she received from her uncle, who seemed to encourage her. Jamas missed Niffy's presence, for the cat generally insinuated herself under any table during dinner. But she was there in his tent when he turned in.

Just before dawn, Niffy awakened Jamas by purring so loudly in his ear he could not ignore her summons. He was up and dressed before a sleepy Grenejon and his valet scratched at the tent door to his quarters.

"Now, Niffy, this is not an occasion for you to ride in the saddlebags," Jamas said, picking her up and handing her firmly to his valet. "Don't let her out of your sight, Arfo, until we're well gone."

"I'll do my best, sire . . ." At which point Niffy squirmed

violently, twisted out of his grasp, and sped across the carpet and out under the tent before anyone could recapture her.

"The most exasperating female I know," Jamas said with more concern than irritation.

"She'll be fine," Grenejon said, starting to shepherd his prince out of the tent, for they could all hear the bustle of men mounting eager horses and the yapping of excited dogs.

"I shall watch out for her, highness," said Arfo. "She will be hungry and return for her breakfast."

Jamas wasn't too sure about that enticement, but he gulped down his early morning brew and chewed on the salt-crusted bread he liked, eager to start the day's business.

Grenejon helped the prince gird on his weapons, plus the crossbow and the several daggers Jamas preferred to carry while hunting, and lastly the heavy gauntlets that fitted snugly to his arm almost to his elbow and the tough leggings that allowed a man to ride through the thickest briars and bushes.

The head forester awaited his prince and the nobles with news of the largest pack of barguas to be seen in the Fial Valley in decades. The hunters gathered about him, keen to start. The man gave a startled glance at the three women of the hunting party and then ignored them.

"Up beyond the waterfall, sire," the man said, pointing in the general direction. "They be harrying the sheep and ibex for it were a hard winter we had and the she-barguas be mighty keen to feed their cubs. One old she-barguas I seen afore, sire, and she be the canniest. Limps she does on her off-fore but that doan' keep her from running well ahead o' any dogs, even thine, nor killing 'em should she be cornered."

The Esphanian barguas-hounds were renowned for their stamina, agility, and intelligence, being not as massive as others bred for this sort of chase. They were especially noted for their cunning in following the merest whiff of barguas-spoor and their tactics when they had cornered one.

"Mount up, then, Bledsoe," the prince said, giving him an approving buffet on the arm before he gestured to the rest of the hunters to get astride.

Jamas' mount this day was a nine-year-old dark dappled gray gelding named Tapper, heavy of bone and tireless, with fine hindquarters that could propel him up the steepest tracks and possessed of courage to spare in confronting barguas, boar, and stag. Grenejon rode a half-brother of the gelding, a bright bay, not a jot less able.

Mounted, Jamas swung Tapper around, automatically checking the other members, and saw all had eschewed yesterday's horses in favor of stockier hunter types. Even Salinah, one crossbow slung across her back and another on the saddle bow, rode a sturdy cob. Willow and Laurel were similarly mounted and carried short, powerful bows and quivers of arrows. The king and most of his group carried the traditional double crossbows as did Jamas' entourage.

"I trust you slept well, Egdril?" Jamas asked, nodding to the three women as he edged his horse close to his guest of honor.

"Like a babe," laughed the king in high humor, glancing eagerly off in the direction he had seen the forester pointing.

"Then let us be off," Jamas said, equally willing to forego further ceremony. He clapped his heels to Tapper's sides, and the gray leaped forward, showing a burst of speed that surprised everyone.

Forester Bledsoe came up just behind the two rulers, pointing his riding stick to show all the way. The kennelmen released the dogs, who quickly forged ahead of the horses, loping in their unmistakable ground-eating pace. When the track took them into the forest, they did not slow down as they had to wend their way around trees and bushes too tall for them to leap.

Egdril was a hard rider, keeping right up to Jamas so that they were stirrup to stirrup.

Then the hounds caught a scent and the chase was on. Down the vale and out of the woods, up the mountain pastures and again into denser forest the dogs led the hunters.

A moment of confusion occurred as the dogs split into several groups. It was obvious to the experienced hunters that the barguas had separated, hoping to lose the dogs on rocky ground.

"Let us do the same," Egdril called to Jamas, and he called out the names of those he wished to take with him.

Jamas did the same but realized that he had acquired two of Egdril's wards: Salinah and Willow. He wasn't going to argue their inclusion, not wishing to waste time. If they could keep up with him, fine. If not, there'd be enough people to direct them back to the lakeside camp. He pushed Tapper on.

Their barguas led them high enough into the rocky terrain that they had to dismount. Salinah and Willow followed him as he started to climb the rocky face. Grenejon was still with him, and one of Egdril's sons, Mavron. The barguas-hounds scrambled ahead, making better use of their four legs than the humans did of two. At the top of that stretch of bare rock, dense forest covered the next slope.

"Careful, my Prince," Grenejon called as they all paused to catch their breaths. "I've been here before and the area is riddled with caves."

"Barguas lead you away from their homeplaces," Salinah said, scornful of his caution.

"From their own homeplaces, Baroness," he said, unslinging his crossbow, "but not from those of another pack. And Bledsoe's report indicated several packs."

"Well, I—"

Several things occurred almost simultaneously. Jamas had just realized that the barguas-hounds were doubling back; he heard a rustling above him; Willow dropped to one knee, her crossbow raised. No sooner had he taken in all this but a gray-brown shape launched itself from a ledge above him and he found himself borne to the ground by the impact of a snarling barguas.

He barely had time to react—crossing his gloved arms to protect his throat from the long sabre-sharp fangs snapping at him. Then he tried to get a grip on the furry ruff and force the barguas's head back, and its snapping jaws away from his most vulnerable spot. The fetid carrion breath of the barguas gagged him. Then, from nowhere, a second and much smaller furry body sprang onto the barguas's muzzle. The wild creature howled as claws sank into its bulging eyes. Then crossbow quarrels smacked into it from three sides.

Protecting Jamas' throat with her own body, Nifry crouched on Jamas' chest on her haunches, both front paws raised, bloodied claws fully extended and ready to strike again as Grenejon grabbed the barguas by the tail and pulled it off his prince.

"I think that kill is mine," Salinah said calmly as she planted one foot on the shoulder to remove her distinctively fletched quarrel from the barguas's right side.

"But you owe your cat your throat, Prince Jamas," Willow

said as she knelt by him. "Are you injured? There's blood . . ." She made exploratory small gestures with her hands on his chest, the side of his neck, without disturbing the vigilant Niffy.

"I think the blood is the barguas's," Jamas said, stroking Niffy who did not move from his chest. "How did you get here, you crazy beast?"

"Here." Salinah reached down to pluck Niffy out of the way.

Niffy turned her head just slightly sideways to hiss at the baroness. The redhead leapt back, drawing her hands protectively in against her body: her expression displaying a sudden anger which she as quickly suppressed with a laugh and a shrug.

"You were very brave, Niffy," Grenejon said, pulling out his crossbow bolt which had gone through the barguas's temples into its brain. He also removed the third quarrel, Willow's, which had entered the barguas's left side, right into the heart. Which of these had actually first killed the barguas was debatable. What was obvious was that Niffy had saved his life.

Shaking off the shock he had sustained from the attack, Jamas pushed himself to a sitting position with one hand, while he hugged Niffy to his chest with the other. She leaped from his restraint and sat a few yards off to lick her paws clean of blood.

"I've never seen anything so brave," Willow said as she dabbed at the few scratches that had broken the skin on Jamas' neck. There were a few beads of blood, but had the barguas's next lunge been unobstructed by the cat, Jamas would have had no throat.

Jamas gently restrained Willow's hand and experienced a

quite remarkable physical shock. That Willow felt it, too, was quite obvious from her sudden intake of breath.

Their eyes met long enough to establish the fact and then instantly they broke contact. Jamas got to his feet and Willow took her quarrel back from Grenejon.

Just then, the rest of their group clambered to the ledge, exclaiming when they saw the dead barguas stretched out in the pine needles. And the dogs reappeared, sniffing and growling at the corpse and acting more as if they had had a part in its death. Niffy was nowhere to be seen.

Following hunting protocol, the forester raised his trumpet to his lips to signal the kill and the sound reverberated from rocky tor to the valleys below. A distant acknowledgment was heard to the north and east of them.

Three more barguas were run during that day; two killed—one by Grenejon and the other by Egdril. The third escaped by making a spectacular leap across a gorge. Mavron told in detail how it had almost lost its hold on the far side before it managed to scramble away into the forest. It had had several arrows in its hide, so it could well be dead of its wounds.

"Formidable predators, these barguas of yours," Egdril remarked, well pleased with the day's chases.

The weary hunters reached the lake as dusk fell: Niffy was back in Jamas' tent before him. Only for the fact that she was sitting on his bed, industriously repairing travel damage to her smoky coat, Jamas would have been hard put to prove that she'd been out of the tent all day.

"Did you know something, Niffy, that you couldn't tell me?" he asked her, starting to slough off his filthy clothes. That was when he noticed a little spot of blood on the coverlet. "Did you hurt yourself?"

She allowed him to feel her all over but pulled away, growling deep in her throat, when he touched one hind leg.

"Now, I'll have no more of that, my dear," he said firmly and found a tear on her right hind leg. *"Grenejon!"*

"My Prince?"

"Get me something to bathe Niffy's paw. She wasn't entirely unscathed."

"Preserve us!" Grenejon left, calling for the groom.

Although the head hostler was also called when Niffy

wouldn't allow Arfo near her, no one was successful. Jamas was worried to the point of fury with his cat.

"You could get an infection! You could be crippled! And it's not an insignificant wound, Niffy. Oh, do be sensible!" Jamas pleaded when angry tones made no impression on his cat, now crouched under his camp bed.

"May I help?" asked the Lady Willow, appearing at the tent door with a small rolled case in her hand. "I tend all my own animals."

So she got down on her stomach, with the others peering under the bed at the recalcitrant Niffy.

"Please? All of you get up and let me try," Willow said. When they had complied, Niffy's ears came forward. "They've gone. Giving you some space, Niffy-cat," Willow said in a sensible voice. Niffy said a surprised "Meh!" at that and relaxed the bristles on her back and tail. "Now, do come out so I can put a little salve on that wound. Barguas wounds so often fester. You owe it to your prince, and to yourself to be treated. You don't want to miss out on tomorrow's hunting, do you?"

"I'm not letting her hunt again . . ." Jamas began.

Willow craned her head up, smiling. "In the first instance, she proved a most valuable ally today against an opponent ten times her size. And in the second, how could you possibly prevent her?"

During this conversation, Niffy emerged from under the bed and, before Jamas could leap to secure her, Willow restrained him and patted the bed for Niffy to jump up. She did, a trifle awkwardly for one of her inherent grace. Then the cat extended her leg for treatment.

"It isn't bad," Willow said, ignoring the men who still anxously crowded about. "Just a tear. On a sharp stone, I shouldn't wonder, so we don't have to worry about barguas saliva. Now, just a dab of this salve, and don't you go licking it off. There now, you'll survive this, too, Niffy-cat, without forfeiting one of your lives."

Once again Niffy said "Meh!" to Willow's style of her name but, so relieved was everyone that the injury was minor, no one noticed. Not even Lady Willow.

As she rolled up her little case of unguents and salves, Jamas sprang forward to offer her his hand and raised her to her feet. If she let her land linger longer in his grasp than was perhaps necessary, only she and Jamas would have known it.

Outside a vigorously clanged bell gave the first warning for the evening meal. Everyone hastened to their quarters to change out of hunting togs.

The hunting party was in good spirits, for they had dispatched three of the marauders and scattered two of the packs—according to he head forester.

Niffy was toasted as a heroine who modestly remained absent, though Jamas ordered that a plate should be prepared for her of the best cuts of the ibex which Egdril had killed shortly after the hunting party had split up.

Laurel sat on one side of Jamas with Salinah on the other, and he accorded them the courtesies without more than a passing glance at the Lady Willow seated with Grenejon and her cousins.

They had even better luck the following day, finding a litter of barguas cubs in one cave and accounting for two males and another nursing female. The hounds also found the arrow-riddled corpse of a fourth adult barguas.

Of course, the fangs were allotted to whichever hunter made the kill. The lesser jaw teeth were still much prized and these were shared out to the huntsmen. The toothless heads of the savage animals looked considerably less ferocious, especially with the protuberant eyes shut. The hides would end up in war shields and vests: nothing was tougher than barguas hide.

The third and fourth day did not provide as much excitement but several more caves were found and the litters dispatched. Not even as cubs were the barguas appealing.

For those keeping track of "finds" and "kills," Esphanian hunters gave the better account but, modestly, Prince Jamas reminded King Egdril that his people were hunting in hills they knew well and so had a slight advantage.

"The point you wished to make, my Prince, has been accepted," Grenejon told Jamas as they reviewed the excursion. "Are they all coming back to the castle with us?"

"Only Egdril and the girls, it seems," Jamas said. His smile broadened as he saw Grenejon's eager expression. "Just the minimum of an honor guard and the necessary servitors. The lads," and he chuckled at the very idea of calling stalwart Geroge and Mavron 'lads,' "will go back to Mauritia with the rest. Egdril didn't wish to strain our hospitality."

"Ha!" The exclamation burst from Grenejon's lips. "What a backhander that is! Or is Egdril enjoying a little joke?"

"I think he must be," Jamas said, his smile fading. "I can't think that he wouldn't know how much older Castle Esphania is than his principal seat in Mauritia. I've sent Arfo on ahead to apprise Frenery. He'll do what's proper."

As indeed Frenery did, though as the secretary bustled about the palace, he, too, missed Mangan, who would have organized everything in a scant hour. He was up half the night with the chatelaine, the head chef, and the equerries who had not gone on the hunting expedition.

The baroness and the Ladies Willow and Laurel were back on their pale horses for the journey to Esphania City. King Egdril was in great good humor as they set out, almost as if he had transferred all the cares of state to his sons. Apart from his honor guard, he brought only two nobles with him, plus his valet and the one maid of his wards who had been willing to accompany them on a hunting expedition.

Egdril was an amusing traveler, asking intelligent questions—if occasionally shrewdly inquisitive—as they made a more leisurely journey back.

He did indeed savor the wines at the hostelry where they partook a light luncheon. The Inn of the Seven Feathers—and, of course, the landlord had to tell that tale which made good listening for the man was a skilled storyteller—was most felicitously placed on the tongue of land that jutted out into the Thuler River, wide at this point as it meandered through the lush flat valley. Spring blossoms still hung on the fruit trees, and the air was loud with industrious bees and other pollinators. They sat at tables on the pleasant court under the spreading paulonia trees, enjoying the sunny weather.

"The very time of year to be out and about," Egdril said

when they were again on their way. "Fine wine, that white. Are your vineyards to the north?"

So Jamas launched into that subject, borrowing heavily from Mangan's frequent discourses on the horticulture closest to his heart.

"You must sample more from the wine cellar," Jamas suggested. "And take home cases of what pleases you."

"A truly royal gift, my young friend."

Behind Jamas, in her saddlebag, Niffy made an odd noise and Jamas realized that Egdril's casual phrase might be considered a portent.

"Of course, since vines do best on south-facing rocky soils, they are inconvenient to access. One must ride onagers to get to most, the trails being winding and dangerous. In fact, if I remember correctly, there's only the one good road to the majority, and nothing more than tracks leading to the vineyards. Still, the caves provide plenty of space for storing the young wines and keep the steady temperature necessary for proper fermentation. Perhaps we can arrange a trip sometime."

Egdril's expression was cheerfully bland as he smiled at Jamas.

"Hmm, yes, sometime."

Salinah took that moment to urge her dainty horse into a race against Grenejon's big bay. Egdril's mount chafed at restraint, and when Willow and Laurel decided to join the race, Jamas did not restrain his stallion, and they all galloped down the track, only pulling up when the city came in sight around the Devil's Elbow. The River Thuler, no longer a placid stream, rushed over its rocky bed in white-watered energy. Of course, the river was responsible for the Elbow in the first place, having carved it from the softer rock.

Out of the corner of his eye, Jamas saw Egdril's shrewd appraisal of that natural fortification. Quite likely the captain of his honor guard was viewing the military aspects of the scenery as closely. Anyone with a modicum of military training could easily see that a dozen men could hold the pass indefinitely. And indeed had done so on quite a few occasions, though the twin forts were now manned only by ceremonial guards. These, resplendent in full dress, lined up on the battlements as the royal party passed. A proper salute was fired, reverberating through the rocky defile—and, incidentally, giving fair warning to the valley beyond.

As often as he approached from this side, Jamas enjoyed the look of Castle Esphania, especially now that the afternoon sun warmed to a golden glow the Esphanian granite. Whereas the castle climbed up the side of the cliff, almost to its summit (which was also fortified), the city spread out past the original walls and down toward the River Thuler.

"You have a truly beautiful city, Prince Jamas," Salinah said beside him.

All the riders pulled their horses back to a walk now. Though the wide road had been beautifully engineered a century before, complete with a stone wall to prevent anyone falling into the river gorge, the sharp cliffs on either side dwarfed its span. The sounds of the horses' hoofs echoed back and forth.

"Clever that," Egdril added, pointing his riding stick up to the heavy nets that kept rocks from tumbling down onto the road.

"Hmm, yes. My great-grandfather designed them," Jamas said, "as he was nearly killed in a rock slide. Things were a little unsettled in those days, too, you may remember, when the empire was dying and some nobles thought to take over the more prosperous of the principalities. Never have used it." Then Jamas added hastily, "But it's regularly checked. Don't wish to have visitors unexpectedly mashed to a pulp." He grinned ingenuously at Egdril, who raised a heavy eyebrow.

Jamas had not sent word that an appropriate official welcome should be laid on, so they entered a city going about its ordinary daily routine. Men saluted him and women curtsied but went on about their business as the royal party made its way up the zigzag roadway to the castle entrance.

By the time they reached the second inner court where Frenery and other courtiers awaited them, Jamas was reasonably sure that Egdril had given up any eagerness for a less friendly visit to Esphania. Or perhaps Jamas misjudged the situation, for the man had brought three very eligible young women with him and there was no doubt that a marital alliance would serve his purpose as well And, if Egdril was allowing Jamas a choice, the prince was not averse to the subtlety. He did want to be able to spend some time with Lady Willow. And as little as possible with Salinah.

Looking around as he dismounted, Jamas caught the almost proprietary look which Salinah was giving the inner court, with its baskets of flowers and ornamental trees.

"Meh!" Niffy said in a definitive tone of voice and extricated herself from the saddlebag.

Mindful of her healing leg, Jamas gently lifted her down, and she streaked away, past the servitors filing out of the side door to attend to horses, luggage and direct the honor guard to their quarters.

Frenery and three only of Jamas' ministerial councillors

had assembled and were now introduced. The whole party was ushered into the smallest of the front reception rooms where beverages and light snacks were being served while luggage was being hurried up to the various bedchambers and apartments.

Then Jamas ushered Egdril to the great Blue Suite, entirely appropriate for a regal visitor, while the chatelaine escorted the girls to the Yellow Rooms. Jamas was amused: those would be more suited to the two brunettes than Salinah. There was, after all, more than one way to deal with such a singleminded young woman.

A ll in all, I think it's going splendidly, Jamie," Grenejon said when they met again in the prince's apartments. Niffy was already there, lounging in the sun as if she hadn't moved a muscle in days.

"Hmmm. I . . . think I agree."

"Only think?" Grenejon stretched out in his favorite chair, long legs crossed at his booted ankles, though he had taken off his spurs which he idly jangled in his free hand. He had poured wine for both of them. Jamas was slowly pacing, head down until he required another sip of his wine. "We've established a good relationship with him and his 'lads', and proved ourselves the better hunters . . ."

"Hunters, yes . . ."

"I shouldn't worry about the rest," Grenejon said with a wave of his spurs. "Not if you agree to marry one of the girls. Have you chosen?"

Jamas gave Grenejon a stern look. Then he hooked his thumb at Niffy. "We'll see."

A state visit would have offered less opportunity for Jamas to get to know the three girls. The evening dinner party, therefore, consisted of Egdril, his nobles and wards, and sufficient Esphanians to make up a proper disposition of men and women. The widowed Duchess of Insaphar, a handsome woman who often acted as Jamas' official hostess, was seated next to King Egdril and could be counted on to entertain him appropriately. Jamas had Grenejon seated next to Salinah while two of Moxtell's sons were seconded to Ladies Willow and Laurel.

However, Jamas planned to have dance music as well as entertainment—the troupe of players was still in the city—after dinner.

He danced with Salinah first, because she required precedence. Then Lady Laurel, who was certainly as skilled a dancer as she was a hunter and made light conversation. Although, later, recalling some odd and ironic comments, Jamas wasn't so certain the conversation was as "light" as it appeared.

Then he allowed himself the indulgence of dancing with Willow. The moment they took hands in the first set, attraction sprang anew between them.

"Please don't, Prince," Willow said, inexplicably distressed. She was smiling up at him, her expression belying her words although the anxiety in her eyes was so intense she was close to tears. "He means you to marry one of us and it will cause your death."

"My lady, how can it? Did he not bring you three lovely ladies along with him for that express purpose? And do we not feel a mutual attraction? Stronger than I have ever felt with any other woman." He tightened his arm about her waist, feeling the lissomeness of her slender body—and thinking thoughts no well-bred man should have of a lady he is dancing with.

"Oh, I do. I do, Jamas. That is why I must warn you. Oh, smile at me, quickly. He's watching."

Jamas complied, laughing lightly as if Willow had said something witty.

"He means to *have* Esphania through such a marriage, and I do not *want* to be part of it."

"Come now, Willow. He can't be such a schemer."

"Oh, he is not, but the queen is!" Through his arms, he could feel her convulsive shudder and saw the haunted look of terror in her eyes. "And if she has a son this time, I worry for my cousins."

Right then, he decided that he would remove that look from her eyes forever.

"I fear my father was murdered for his lands," she said, her mouth smiling as she looked up with anxious eyes at Jamas. "He was too experienced a horseman and an experienced hunter to have misjudged such a critical distance. I would not want the same fate to befall you. Besides," she went on, "surely you were betrothed in your cradle to a northern princess?"

Jamas shook his head. "I am however forewarned, and that is forearmed, dear Lady Willow, for I mean to marry you and remove such fear from your life."

"No, never! I couldn't marry you. I like you too much!" she cried, twisting out of his grasp and whirling away and off the dance floor.

"I love you, too, Lady Willow," he said in a loud enough voice to stop the music and cause everyone to stare at him.

Salinah, partnered with one of the Moxtell sons, glared furiously after Willow's disappearing figure. Egdril beamed and started forward, hand outstretched, evidently all too eager to acknowledge a relationship. Grenejon looked flabbergasted, the duchess surprised, Moxtell amazed, and all the others merely gawked. It was the white face and haunted eyes of Laurel which caught Jamas' gaze: it confirmed what Willow had said.

Then Jamas had to apologize to Egdril for his presumption, but the king dismissed it, beaming with delight that one of his "girls" had so captured the prince's interest. A sparkling wine was ordered and there was much drinking of toasts, and healths, and— ironically, under the circumstances—long happy lives.

The duchess went to fetch Willow from the walled garden to which she had fled. She had no escape, either, from the public announcement of his love for her. Laurel, still pale, with lips closed over her own sentiments, sat close by her sister, Jamas on the other side. Frenery was sent for and apprised of the engagement. Though initially astounded, the old secretary expressed the proper sentiments and promised to have a betrothal document drawn up by the morrow.

If the newly betrothed lady seemed stunned and kept very quiet, the prospective groom was voluble enough for both. He kept his lady's hand firmly in his.

They danced again and again until Lady Willow pleaded a headache and was allowed to retire with her sister.

The rest of the small party continued to celebrate until well into the new day.

S o, my prince?" Grenejon asked when he firmly closed the door to make them private in Jamas' apartments, "why does the blushing bride look as if she is going to her death rather than her wedding?"

"Not her death, mine," Jamas said, sighing with relief as he loosened the collar of his formal tunic. He succinctly repeated what Willow had told him.

"You're mad, Jamie," and Grenejon collapsed into a chair, his face as pale as Willow's had been, "walking right into such a trap. Did not Mangan teach you better? And don't tell me you're madly in love or some such nonsense. Argh!"

Niffy bounded into the room, looking from one to the other, before she leaped to her prince's shoulder and stroked his cheek.

"Niffy approves."

"Niffy?" Grenejon dismissed approval from that quarter. "Now, that's adding folly to stupidity!"

"Don't be so patronizing, Gren. I'm going to rely heavily on Niffy's special sensitivities."

"On the cat's?" Niffy said a distinct "Meh!" in Grenejon's direction, and he blinked. "Saving you from a barguas is quite a different matter to saving you from the connivance of an ambitious and murderous queen."

"Ah, but forearmed is forewarned, Gren, and you shall discover as discreetly as possible how these various nobles met their untimely ends."

"As if that would prevent yours! I mean, Willow's a lovely girl, but there are many lovely girls . . ."

"She has more than beauty, Grenejon," Jamas said stiffly, flexing hands that remembered the exciting touch of her. "She likes cats, and Niffy approves. Don't you?" He turned his face into the cat's fur and heard the loud rumble of her purr.

"You are mad, Jamas!" Grenejon repeated, rising to his feet. "Mad, mad, mad!"

"Yes, I am. Mad that my Willow should be put in such a position. And I wouldn't marry Salinah were I you. Your estate could be neatly absorbed into Egdril's kingdom, you know."

"Oh, I've already decided the Baroness Salinah wouldn't give me much connubial bliss!" Grenejon said, flinging those hands over his head in an expansive gesture as he paced in front of Jamas. "She would possibly accept a prince, but not a baron. She's infected with the same ambitions as her step-aunt. But you . . . you're the ruler of Esphania. We need you alive!"

"I'll live. I assure you." Jamas stroked Niffy, pleased at the fervor of his friend's concern.

Grenejon kept up his arguments even after the betrothal agreement was signed. Without mentioning it to his prospective uncle-in-law, Prince Jamas also signed a succession document, copies of which were lodged with his General of the Army, all his ministers, Moxtell, Earl of Oria, the Duke of Insaphar, and the Fennells. They couldn't object to his second cousin, since the youngster was young enough to be moulded, as he had been, for the princedom.

Egdril was further delighted when Prince Jamas insisted on a short engagement and asked for the wedding to be scheduled as soon as feasible.

A brief impasse occurred when Egdril said that he preferred the nuptials to take place in Mauritia.

"Ah, I wish I could concede to that point," Jamas said with a heavy sigh, "but I am prince of Esphania and owe my own citizens the pleasure of such a fine occasion."

Egdril marshalled quite a few arguments for Mauritia, most based on the fact that the wedding party—if it included all who must, or should, be invited—might tax Esphania's facilities.

Jamas laughed merrily, while Frenery and Grenejon hastily cleared their throats. As the men were seated in one of the smaller reception rooms—which could easily accommodate a full orchestra and two hundred dancing couples plus attendants—the contention had little merit.

"I shall allot the west wing to your majesty's immediate relations," Jamas said, with an airy wave of his hand towards that massive annex, "and I think we can comfortably house a few extra hundred without putting a strain on my resources."

Afterwards, Grenejon taxed Jamas with that bit of bravado.

"He'll want Castle Esphania even more now."

"Let him 'want' away," Jamas said, still elated at having had his way on what he considered major issues.

The next morning King Egdril eagerly prepared to set off for home, though messengers had carried the glad tidings to Mauritia the morning after that auspicious evening. Jamas and Willow didn't get much time together, and he had occupied the stolen moments in loving attentions which indeed she accepted and returned in spite of her fears. Jamas was rather pleased with his effect on her. Not to mention hers on him. Egdril was still doing more planning for the wedding than Jamas wanted done. But it was wise to allow Egdril to rattle on about country estates and dower provisions. Jamas knew how far he intended to go in this regard and would not be moved. Mangan had instructed him well in the art of negotiation.

"I've a fine galleon for you to use should you decide on an ocean voyage for your honeymoon," Egdril said as he settled himself in the saddle for his journey home.

"Why, that is most gracious, Egdril," Prince Jamas said, trying to control the eagerness of the royal handshake. He released himself before his arm dropped off and stepped back as a discreet signal that Egdril should finally leave.

"And if you drowned on your honeymoon?" Grenejon whispered in his ear as the royal party clattered out of the courtyard. "Laurel gave me all the details we need about sudden deaths among Mauritian nobles. You'll want to hear them. Clever. All occurring *after* the ungood second wife married Eager Egdril, all different, all easily explicable, and all eight men just as dead as the next one."

"Elucidate," Jamas said as he led Grenejon back to his office where he was going to look over the ancestral jewels with a view to resetting those most likely to suit Willow's dark beauty.

"Baron Ricaldo was a fine horseman and the stallion he was riding could have leaped a ravine twice the width of the one they were found in. Found halfway across, in fact. As if something had caused the horse to misjudge the leap or have a sudden heart attack. They seem to have dropped like a couple of stones. Considering the depth of the ravine, it was difficult to disentangle the mashed corpses."

"He was the first?"

"Yes, Willow's father. He didn't much like Queen Yasmin but then he had gained much favor from Egdril by finding him eager and willing bedmates." Grenejon grinned lasciviously. "The second one took longer. Duke Kesuth began to experience nausea and nothing could ease his discomfort. Or permit him to retain any food. You might say he died of starvation."

"Poison is often the tool of females," Jamas said, waving at Grenejon to close the door behind him.

Niffy was sitting in the sun on his desk—on the list of wedding guests, to be precise, beside the flat velvet boxes and leather cases that held the ancestral jewelry.

"No poison could have that effect, or so I'm informed," Grenejon said.

"Go on."

"Admittedly, shipwrecks are hard to arrange because storms at sea are chancy, but Count Lansaman was an accomplished sailor and quite capable of managing his sloop in the roughest weather. He and all hands, including—this is significant—both his heirs perished in waters too deep to raise their vessel."

"Now that would have taken some doing, Gren. Arranging a storm at a propitious moment. We don't have many practicing sorcerers with that capability."

"Hmm. That we know of," Grenejon said pointedly. "However, let me note that Lansaman was Egdril's chief financial advisor, and he thought that the king shouldn't spend money building a pleasure garden for the queen when a larger hospital was urgently needed. So he drowned."

"Go on."

"Count Mataban did not wish to betroth his daughter to Egdril's choice for her—to one of the Bosanavian kinglets."

"I should think not," and Jamas shuddered, "living in felt tents on the move all the time *and* in that frightful climate. So what happened to Mataban?"

"He was attacked in his own gardens—he was an ardent horticulturist—by an assassin."

"A renegade Bosanavian who had taken offense to the slight?" Jamas suggested.

"Exactly, and the man was found hanged in his cell before he could be questioned."

"If, indeed, the queen is responsible, she's thorough and . . . tidy."

"And you're prepared to marry into jeopardy?"

"I'm marrying Lady Willow, not her step-aunt."

"Who, after she's heard the report on the amenities of Esphania, is very likely to wish to annex it to Mauritia."

"We are forewarned. What of the rest of them?" Jamas asked.

Grenejon ticked them off on his fingers. "One unexpectedly killed in a tourney. Another was done in out hunting by a particularly savage female lynzur. There aren't *that* many lynzurs left in our world. Another had a heart attack, and the last developed a debilitating ague and died of fever."

"And nothing common amongst them . . ."

"Save that the queen liked none of them for one reason or another."

"And you think I'll be . . . put down . . . as easily?" Jamas laughed but Grenejon frowned angrily.

"I don't think 'easy' applies, my Prince. But I'm going to take a few safeguards. Like this." Grenejon held up a heavy silver ring of simple but elegant design: a flat cut peridot sparkled brightly. "The stone changes color when in proximity to any known poison." He took Jamas' right hand and slipped the ring on the forefinger. "Just where it will be close to any food you eat and any drink you drink without everyone knowing you are protected by the sigil."

Jamas was deeply touched by Grenejon's thoughtfulness as well as the gift itself. It fit his finger as if it had always been there.

"I've got the armorer making you the finest mesh, capable of deflecting arrow or dagger . . . at least long enough for you to grab your own knife. And the kennel master has been training a barguas-hound to sleep in your room . . ."

"You know I don't like dogs in my bedroom. Besides which, Niffy is quite enough of a private guard."

"We shall guard your every minute, my Prince," his equerry said staunchly, his back straight and his jaw obstinate.

"Not every minute, surely, Grenejon." And the prince winked.

J amas! Please be sensible!" the Baron Illify roared.

Niffy meowed.

"You see? She's volunteered for the other minutes," Jamas said and gave her an affectionate caress before he started to open the jewelry boxes. "Now, help me decide which of these Willow will like?"

"You should do the wedding guest list first," Grenejon said.

"What? And disturb Niffy when she's so comfortable? No, we do jewels first, then we'll get on with the notables."

They got on with both tasks. The jewels were sent to be reset or cleaned, and the invitations were dispatched: many by special couriers. The replies flooded back almost by return of the post riders. So heavy was the traffic of heralds— as if folks feared a late response would deprive them of their designated places—that guards had to direct the flow in and out of the castle gates, which had previously always been adequate for daily traffic.

The church was cleaned from belfry to crypt—not, Grenejon remarked, that anyone (and he nodded significantly at his prince) was likely to visit such a malodorous and doleful place.

"You never know," remarked Cambion, the second equerry called in to assist his prince and Grenejon. "When m'sister got married last year, we found knickers and stuff for weeks afterwards." When he saw the severe expressions on the faces of prince and head equerry, he blushed and hastily added, "Of course, at a royal wedding . . ."

"There will be far more discards and in far more unlikely places," Jamas said, keeping his expression so stern that for another long moment, Cambion didn't realize he was being teased.

Riding about in the city, Jamas found himself amused and pleased by the energy of the inhabitants, all determined that no one could find fault with any household or public place. Not a hovel was left un-freshened with limewash, and larger buildings had their masonry scrubbed by diligent teams. Baskets of flowers hung from street lamps, and corners or front windows sported at least a bright potted plant.

"I should get married more often," Jamas remarked when he saw special feeding stations erected well away from the cathedral plaza so that pigeons would be enticed from their usual haunts and not soil the wedding crowds.

Once the traffic of speedy replies slackened, carters and carriers arrived with wedding presents. The third largest reception room joined the second to display the gifts pouring in from both kingdoms. Some, of course, had to be refrigerated in the icecaves which were already preserving wedding feast supplies. Others met with some ridicule, and there were dozens of duplicates, but as some of these were useful items, the donors received gracious thanks.

The bride and her entourage arrived a good ten days before the wedding, with such a baggage train that Cambion was heard to remark aloud that he hoped there would be enough closets in the west wing for everything.

She's not coming," was the first sentence Lady Willow whispered in the ear of her intended.

"Oh?" Jamas held his fiancée slightly away from him, looking into her eyes to see if there was a diminution of her anxiety. Despite the dark circles under them, he thought she looked marginally less tense.

"She *is* pregnant and will not trust herself to being jostled in a coach." Willow paused a beat. "She made my own mother stay behind with her and sent her sister along." Willow actually wrinkled her nose up at him. "To act on behalf of both. It was mean of her to keep my own mother, even if Mother is very good with gestational vapors." Willow sighed with regret. "At least I was allowed Laurel."

"Ah, Lady Laurel," Jamas said, taking the hand of his sister-in-law elect and pulling her into his side to give her an affectionate kiss.

"Don't think you're marrying the pair of us," Laurel said with a little laugh, but his attention had pleased her for her eyes sparkled.

Then Jamas noticed that she was surveying the assembled. Her eyes became focused and he saw that she had been looking for Grenejon.

The equerry, who had been giving directions to a stylishly dressed older woman, hurried to his prince and the two ladies.

"Lady Willow, your obedient and faithful servant," Grenejon said with a deep and respectful bow which he then turned in Lady Laurel's direction. "I am yours equally, Lady Laurel. Countess Solesne is anxious to whisk you both away to your apartments to rest."

Willow let out an exasperated sigh. "I have never fainted in my life, and I am certainly not fatigued by the journey. Sollie does worry that I won't be in looks on The Day." Her voice was almost merry but then her face clouded as she saw who was approaching their quartet from the other large travelling coach. She laid her hand on Jamas' arm, her fingers pressing fiercely. "Prince Jamas, may I make known to you, Fanina, Duchess of Glebes?"

Jamas was seized with an intense desire to say, "No, you may not!" as the small, very elegant lady swayed daintily toward him. She was not unattractive but there was something about the expression in her face or the set of her eyebrows or the masculine squareness of her jawline that was somehow repellent. Or maybe it was the acquisitive squint with which she surveyed the courtyard. Jamas raised her from her graceful but shallow curtsey—his rank, if not hers, decreed a fuller obeisance—and wanted to rub his fingers of the moisture left there by her plump little hand.

"My brother at law, Egdril, King of Mauritia, will be here shortly," she said in carefully precise vowels. "He decided to ride through this charming little city."

I t's not *little*," Cambion complained later when they reviewed the arrival. "And to announce him like that! She's not a chamberlain or anything. To act as if we wouldn't know who he was or where he came from!"

Grenejon suggested that she either had a speech impediment which her careful enunciation was covering or that she had learned the language late in life.

"I'd bet she came from a very humble origin and had a dreadful twang," was Jamas' notion.

However, on the steps of the castle, he had to prolong the welcoming ceremonies until Egdril and his honor guard clattered into the court and could be officially greeted.

The countess had taken her charges away to the west wing, and the prince and his equerries perforce had to exchange pleasantries with Duchess Fanina. This was not easily done, for she came across as a contentious, critical, patronizingly unpleasant person, and there were many long pauses between comments, with prince and first equerry sharpening their ears for any sound of the approaching royal troop.

Egdril finally charged into the courtyard with his royal honor guard, and Jamas almost embraced him for rescuing them from Fanina. Jamas was not the only one to notice that Egdril didn't much like his relative by marriage. But protocol was acquitted and they could begin the festivities concomitant with such a felicitous occasion.

If Jamas thought he'd have much of his fiancée's company,

he thought wrong. They still had to steal moments together—generally on the dance floor—to the point where Countess Solesne was heard to remark that she hadn't ever seen the Lady Willow dance so often.

Duty required Prince Jamas to take Duchess Fanina to the dance floor at least once. Although it was the custom for ladies to wear gloves at formal dance evenings, she did not. He had to take her plump moist hands in his. That was the first time the ring changed color. Immediately after he had seen her to her chair, he excused himself and scrubbed his hands vigorously until his ring resumed its normal shade.

"Know much about contact poisons, Gren?" he murmured to his equerry at the next available moment.

Grenejon's eyes rounded. "Since I don't, I shall repair that ignorance. Mangan had a full library on such affairs, I believe."

Jamas noticed enviously that his equerry was able to leave the dance floor with the Lady Laurel. Whenever he and Willow tried the same maneuver, someone followed them: the countess, Egdril, the duchess, Frenery, or *someone*.

"I've only kissed you four times since you got here," Jamas said, holding the slender body of his intended tightly in his arms. That wasn't as satisfactory, in some ways, as kissing her, but evidently it would have to do. He found he could put a lot of loving in such an embrace in front of all the eyes on them.

"We shall have some time together soon," she said, her body answering his.

He smiled down at her. "So you do love me?"

"More than I thought possible," she replied fervently, and he sighed. Seven more days until he had her to himself, legally and irrefutably.

The days eventually passed, and he was being dressed in his wedding finery, resplendent with gold and silver in the vibrant dark green that was Esphania's color.

"You look every inch a fine prince, Jamie," Grenejon said, brushing off an imaginary speck from his shoulders.

"You're not at all shabby either," Jamie replied, for Gren wore an equerry's formal dark blue with a modest silver trim. "Is all in train?"

Grenejon winked, grinning from ear to ear, and patted his left slit pocket.

A polite tap sounded on the door, which Grenejon opened to Prince Temeron, who looked excessively nervous and obviously uncomfortable in his finery. He also looked remarkably like his cousin, the prince, which was somewhat natural since they were closely related. They were the same height and build, Temeron being younger by some eighteen months. But his blond hair curled—and had been barbered—like the prince's, and their profiles were much of a kind.

"Tern, you look splendid," Jamas said, striding forward to shake his second cousin's hand and reassure the lad. Temeron had not yet been informed that he was now the crown prince although Jamas had decided the boy had better leave his ancestral home, high in the northern mountains, and get eased into Esphania court procedures and policies.

"Came to tell you we're all assembled now, sir . . ."

"Jamas, lad, Jamas," the prince reminded him, and Tern

blushed. He had been seconded as a groomsman along with the Moxtell sons and brothers, Grenejon's two younger brothers, and the Fennells.

Swinging the door wide open, Jamas looked out at the colorful assembly for each wore his family's heraldic colors. Every one of them was six foot or more and athletic in appearance. Even Temeron had a martial bearing.

"We'll make a fine show," he said, nodding approval.

"A fine show indeed," Grenejon murmured for the prince's hearing alone and chuckled.

"Easy now, the doing's yet to be done," and with that the Prince of Esphania strode forth to his wedding.

Awedding is a wedding, and that of a popular prince is even more an occasion for rejoicing. This wedding also included the prince's official coronation and that of his bride. Fortunately, he could and had chosen the short forms so he could get to the important part of his wedding sooner. Everyone in Esphania was there, except Niffy, who had other plans for this day.

The bride arrived precisely on time, on her uncle's arm, looking so ethereal in her gauzy dress and lacy veil that Jamas thought his heart would burst. He was not ashamed to find tears in his eyes.

It seemed to take forever for the procession to bring her to him, for she had twelve attendants and two flower girls and two lads bearing on one pillow the rings and on the other the coronets. Jamas eyed the two boys most severely. They were the sons of Duchess Fanina, and obnoxious little scuts, or so he had found out when he caught them mercilessly mistreating puppies in his stable. They rolled their eyes when they saw him watching and started taking their duties more seriously.

Then, finally, King Egdril bestowed the Lady Willow's hand in his. Lady Laurel took her place beside her sister and Grenejon, as best man, turned by his prince. What no one else but the participants and the celebrant knew was that this was a double wedding ceremony: Laurel had agreed to Gren's persuasions.

The ceremony, with Willow's slender fingers tightly clasping Jamas', seemed to be over all too soon, and he was kissing his bride. Grenejon would have to wait to perform that ritual when the wedding party retired to the chancel to sign the register, but Bishop Wodarick had accepted their whispered responses to the usual wedding vows. If his blessing was more expansive, taking in the other pair, no one noticed it particularly.

As best man, of course, Grenejon had to escort the maid of honor, and that was when they exchanged their rings.

Back out, with only a quick sip of wine to sustain them through the next part of the ceremony, and Jamas and Willow were crowned Prince and Princess of Esphania.

The oaths of fealty from the nobles were limited to the Duke of Brastock as the oldest of the nobles, the Earl of Moxtell, Count Fennell, and Baron Illify, all swearing allegiance to prince and princess on behalf of others of their rank. The Lord Mayor of Esphania City handled the one for the citizenry.

Then, the congregation—already on their feet—let out the traditional cheers as the prince and princess made their way down the aisle and to the waiting carriage.

In the very next coach rode Grenejon and Lady Laurel, to the consternation of Duchess Fanina, who thought she and her brother-in-law should have been the next passengers. Egdril, with a little help from Moxtell, Fennell, and Brastock, smoothed the whole thing over.

Fanina's expression suggested that she would have a word or two with the impudent best man and maid of honor—though somehow or other, she never did.

The wedding feast would go down in Epicurean annals for that decade. The subtleties were fantastic, the viands incredible—especially considering the numbers who dined. Frenery had outdone himself—as had the leading citizens of

Esphania who had been unstinting in the supplies of food, the labor required, and in general the organization, so that everyone within the city, be they guest, resident, or innocent traveller, ate to satiation that night.

If the guests in the castle banqueting hall also noticed that the prince and princess fed each other from a single plate and drank from a single cup, it was considered "sweet" and "loverly." Though why Duchess Fanina frowned so much was not immediately apparent.

"They dare not poison me, too, you see," Willow murmured to her brand new husband.

"Do stop fretting, my love . . ."

"You simply won't believe me," Willow said with a tremulous note in her voice.

He folded his hand around her fingers. "I do, love, I do. And have taken steps to ensure my continued existence. Please, my love, at least enjoy your sister's wedding." He smiled mischievously at her.

"Oh, you!" and she started to laugh, glancing over her shoulder at Grenejon and Laurel, who were observing more decorous behavior in their manner of eating.

Before there could be the dancing which Jamas looked forward so much to, there were the toasts and the speeches to be sat through. But Frenery had had severe notice from his prince to limit these as much as possible. Only King Egdril, waffling on about the union between the two great nations, did not observe the restriction. But then, no one had mentioned it to him.

At last, when the chamber group was augmented by the full orchestra which would play dance music, the prince and his princess retired briefly so that she could remove her cumbersome train for dancing. They, of course, had the first dance, in which they acquitted themselves to the onlookers' delight. If Princess Willow had resumed her veil, no one thought it odd. The prince handed his partner to her uncle and bowed before Duchess Fanina, adjusting his white gloves before he took her hand. Two circles of the floor and the Duke of Moxtell requested the pleasure of Duchess Fanina's company, and the prince relinquished her with a show of reluctance. And, shucking the gloves off his hands, he deposited them behind a plant. Few noticed that it wilted and died that night.

Then everyone started dancing and, if the prince slipped off for a moment, he was back on the floor very shortly, claiming a dance with each bridesmaid in turn. If he did not appear as graceful in these turns as he usually did, by then there had been sufficient wine drunk that it passed unnoticed.

Indeed it was fairly late into the evening that people began to realize that they had not seen the princess dancing, nor Baron Illify and Lady Laurel. And when the Duchess Fanina archly told her brother-in-law, the king, that it was time to bed the happy couple, it was Egdril who noticed that the "prince" was really Prince Temeron, dressed in his cousin's finery, who had been partnering the bridesmaids. As these young ladies were all from Mauritia, they had not recognized the deception.

"Well, you see, your majesty," Temeron began, casting about to find Frenery or Moxtell or someone of greater rank than he held to support him in this explanation, "my cousin, Prince Jamas, is not a great one for ceremony and the, ah, um . . ."

"Bedding," Moxtell put in, arriving to assist the inexperienced courtier.

"Yes, that was one he particularly wanted to avoid."

The Duchess Fanina did not speak but, almost as if the movement was being choreographed, those nearest her moved back, leaving her isolated in a small empty circle.

"One could almost feel the heat of her anger," Temeron later told his cousin. "She was really, really mad."

Jamas only laughed and thanked his cousin again for standing in for him.

The king was not best pleased about this unexpected departure and shirking of "dynastic duty" but Brastock and Moxtell managed to jolly him out of his displeasure. And one of the Fennell daughters was only too happy to dance with him . . . all night long. And, as it happened, as long as he was in Esphania, which did not make him eager to return to his moody pregnant wife.

Meanwhile both couples had made good their escape: Baron and Baroness Illify to his estate and the Prince and Princess of Esphania to a long-unused but newly refurbished lodge high up on the Elbow. Jamas' great-grandfather had used it when overseeing the construction of the landslide nets.

"It's the last place in the principality anyone would think to look for us," Jamas told his wife as he handed her down from the dark mare. "The fire needs only the touch of a match inside," he added as he took the horses to the lean-to to tend them.

When he entered, he found the fire was burning merrily and Willow leaning against the thick log mantel, watching the flames. She gave a little start as the door snicked shut and Jamas dropped the bar in place.

"No one will find us here, my love," he said, glancing about to see that his requirements had been met: the table set with its two places and covered dishes, wine in a cooler, flowers and garlands lending their own scent to the freshness of the newly done room. He must reward Cambion who had done the work—most of it by himself.

"Then at least we'll have had this," she said in a brief return of her fatalistic attitude.

He pulled her in very close embrace, and she responded as ardently as he had hoped she might.

"Worry later, my love. Tonight is ours! I love you so much,

my Willow Princess." And he proceeded to demonstrate how much.

P rince Jamas delayed returning to the city until King Egdril and especially that awful Duchess Fanina had wearied of waiting for the newlyweds to return and gone back to Mauritia. Six days after their arrival at the lodge, a note was added to the supplies discreetly deposited on the porch of the lodge.

"Queen sent messenger for king. He leaves this morning. Will send escort for Lady Laurel. They think the baron and she are with you."

Jamas chuckled and even Willow smiled happily.

"You weren't looking forward to seeing him again, were you?"

Willow gave a little shudder. "I don't mind my uncle. It's the duchess who's almost as bad as her sister."

"You're safe now."

"And my uncle hasn't realized that Laurel's not going back?"

"Evidently not. But, don't worry, she's now my sister-in-law, you know, as well as the wife of my first equerry. And we protect our own!" He gave her a squeeze.

"He mightn't do anything," Willow said, "but *she* might. I know she had plans for Laurel, you see."

"Marrying her off to a Gorundian hairy monster?" Jamas said jokingly.

"Almost." Willow gave a flicker of a smile. "I worry about my mother, though, and our younger sisters . . ."

"Do I have to find brides for all of them?" And he quickly

added, when he saw that his flippancy wounded her, "and I will, of course, should you wish me to."

"I'd rather they were far away from Mauritia when Laurel's marriage is discovered."

"Done," and Jamas kissed her. "Hmm . . . It'll take the royal party five days with those heavy coaches to make it back to Mauritia. And before they get there, your mother and sisters will be safely ensconced elsewhere and under my protection."

Returning by horseback, the keen-eyed Elbow guard sent word of the imminent arrival of the prince and princess. So the happy couple were greeted by showers of cheers and rose petals as they made their way through the city to the castle. Someone had also apprised Frenery and he was there to greet them, looking immensely relieved.

"A discreet task for you, Frenery," Jamas said, tak-ing his secretary by the arm into the nearest private room.

"Oh dear." Frenery wrung his hands.

"Dear Frenery, what discreet tasks have you had to do recently that put you in such a tizzy?"

"Oh dear!" Frenery repeated, blushing furiously.

"My uncle," Willow said in a dry tone.

"Never mind him," Jamas said, not quite realizing what his lovely bride was implying. "My mother-in-law—" He smirked a bit. "—needs to be spirited out of King Egdril's palace, and my wife's younger sisters quietly abducted from their home in . . . where do they live, Willow?"

"On the Farm in Yolend. It's not far from Mauritia City. And they're all good riders."

"All? How many sisters-in-law do I have now?" Jamas was surprised.

"Three, including Laurel, but I meant that Mother rides well, too, and it's much easier riding than disappearing by coach."

"Indeed it is. Will you see to it, Frenery? The Moxtell lads would do the job neatly enough and the Earl's old barn of a castle can suffice until I can set up a more suitable residence for them."

"Oh, dear, oh dear."

"What is the matter, Frenery?"

"The Countess Solesne. I thought she'd gone. I handed her into the coach myself but she's here. In your quarters, with Cambion."

"Oh dear," and now Princess Willow took up the chorus, gathering up her riding skirt and running out of the little salon and up the stairs, the prince following her after telling Frenery to set the rescue in train.

The countess was attended by a very nervous Cambion.

"She insisted on staying," the lad said.

"What is it, Sollie? You should be safe enough," said Willow, rushing to embrace her old friend.

"I would be," Sollie said, rising, "only I heard a conversation which I must inform you of, or I could never live with my conscience. But, first, is there any way you can get your dear mother and sisters out of Mauritia?"

"That's already taken care of," Jamas said, feeling rather superior at the moment. "Now, what could possibly prey upon the conscience of a woman of your integrity, Countess?"

"Murder," she said, looking him straight in the eye.

"Heavens, above! Whose?" The prince motioned for her to resume her seat.

"Yours, your highness," she said, tilting her head to regard him as if she was certain he would doubt her.

"Oh, dear! I knew it!" Willow turned tragic eyes to Jamas.

"Now, love," and Jamas drew his wife to him and then gently pushed her onto the love seat. He beckoned for Cambion to serve them all wine. "Tell me, Countess."

"I overheard them, the countess and that sourfaced maid of hers," Sollie began when she had taken a sip of wine. "Oh!" as Niffy leaped to the top of the table beside her. The countess, not being a cat lover, nonetheless instantly stroked the silky head of this most unusual feline.

"Do go on . . ." Jamas urged.

Satisfied by the attention, Niffy then leaped down and up into what little space there was on the couch between the newlyweds, purring softly and turning her green almond-shaped eyes on Sollie's woeful face.

"I don't think they know that I did, but I heard them discuss . . . ways and means . . ." She shuddered and took another sip. "I know you have discounted Willow's fears, sir, but they are real. Too many of us in Mauritia live in fear of . . . that woman! And Fanina!" The countess almost spat the name out. "By any chance, did you happen to notice how moist her hands are?" When Jamas nodded, she went on. "I have reason to believe she transfers a subtle slow poison in that fashion."

"I, too," and Jamas twisted his finger around so that Sollie could see the jewel he wore. "This detects poisons."

"Oh, you did listen to me," Willow said, relief taking away the strain about her eyes.

Niffy very distinctly said, "Meh."

"And you told him, too, did you, Niffy-cat?" Willow said, stroking her lavishly.

"Did you wash your hands instantly?" Sollie asked the prince.

"Until the jewel returned to its proper shade," Jamas said. "But how could a single exposure affect me?"

"It's cumulative," Sollie said. "I know you had to dance

with her at the wedding dinner . . ."

"I wore gloves. Specifically for dancing with her."

"Wise! If you also discarded them the moment you could? Oh, good. You were very wise. That sort of poison can filter through cloth as easily as it does flesh. Now, there are other ways in which this tactile poison can be transferred to the intended victim," Sollie went on. "You will probably discover some new apparel in your closet, gifts from your generous relatives. I know of a solution in which these items can be washed . . . for you may be sure that if you are not seen to wear them, that information will be passed back to Mauritia."

"They left spies behind?"

"I believe there have been a few in place here in Esphania for some time, your highness," the countess added as she took a small packet of notes out of her reticule and handed over the first sheet. "The recipe for the solution—all relatively common substances. This," and she passed over another sheet before Jamas had a chance to read the first, "is another contact poison that is soaked into things as innocent as the brushes you use on your hair, the stick you carry to ride, your favorite saddle, your usual chair. Minute portions, but gradually, daily contact would put enough in your body to be effective."

"Duke Kesuth?" Jamas asked.

"I fear so," Sollie said with a sigh. "And Willow's father, too. For why else would such a capable man, and such a strong fine horse, have such a bizarre accident?" She reached over to pat Willow's hand, for the reminder saddened the princess. "I think now that they believe they have set such . . . arrangements . . . in place, they will wait to hear of sudden indispositions of the Prince of Esphania."

"And my unexpected demise at an early age?" Jamas

asked, pulling his mouth down in a suitably lugubrious smile, though his eyes danced. When the countess nodded solemnly, he asked, "And how long should that take?"

Sollie shrugged. "We've never been able to estimate that because we never knew *when* the victims were first . . . ah . . . poisoned but you are a young, healthy man and would not succumb too easily."

"Your queen has been a very busy woman, has she not?"

The countess gave another little shudder. "Endlessly. One never knows what she'll do next. I have observed that the queen enjoys scheming and is always positive that others are so involved. As if we all had her greed for power."

"My, she is a virago!" Jamas gave a mock shudder of fear.

"Do not underestimate her," princess and countess said simultaneously.

"Oh, I do not," Jamas assured them. "Cambion, what new apparel has reached my wardrobes? Would you know?"

"I do, indeed, my Prince, for I put the packages in a separate place for you to inspect at your convenience even before I had any notion the contents might put you in danger."

"All right." Jamas handed Cambion the recipe for the antidotal solution. "Get Frenery to collect these items." Niffy merowed. "Oh? They might be in Mangan's possession? Hmm, that will make it even simpler. Cambion, you have just been promoted to launderer. Would they have dusted my boots, d'you think?"

"Not only your boots but every shoe you own," Sollie said firmly to counteract his levity. "They even mentioned how leather holds the poison better than cloth. Your feet, when warmed by even such minor exercise as walking, would absorb more that way."

"As well that my shoemaker has my last fitting and can make replacements for all my footwear."

And so they planned to combat the threat. The countess was spirited through the secret passageways to Mangan's tower where, with Cambion, she made safe the new garments—rather beautifully embroidered shirts—which Jamas then wore whenever possible.

"But where will Sollie go?" Willow asked when the first excitement of their counter-deception was complete. "I mean, the tower is lovely but is it safe?"

"Safe enough for the nonce, but perhaps she would enjoy the freedom of our honeymoon lodge? That is not only isolated but protected by the Elbow guard detachment."

"Oh," and Willow's face was wistful.

"Ah, then, you don't like to think of anyone using our retreat?" Jamas wound a strand of her silky black hair around his finger. And laughed when she blushed. "Then I shall think of another refuge."

"Is there not a place in the city itself . . ."

"A good idea. Hide something where it is most visible. No one need remark on a widow, possibly slightly infirm, taking a house in a quiet square, now would they? I know the very one." Jamas gave the orders to Cambion, who had not thought to have so many diverse tasks as his prince's aide. "And you, my love, will still have the good countess nearby until your mother is safely within our boundaries, too."

The young equerry had made so much use of the secret passageways that he knew almost as many as his prince and Grenejon did. So he made all the arrangements through an intermediary and even employed his younger brother as the "grandson" of the elderly widow because, as he told his prince, "Simon is so close-mouthed, he never says two words when a nod or a shrug will suffice."

The prince was breaking in his new boots when an officer of the guard requested entry.

"My Prince," and he brought his right fist smartly across his chest in a thumping salute, "a small company of men, Prince Mavron at their head, have just received permission to pass through the Elbow."

"On, indeed? Did they vouchsafe why they are coming on this visit?"

"To collect Lady Laurel for her imminent wedding!"

Jamas was as glad that Willow was with her ladies or she would lose all the self-confidence she had acquired in her married life.

"How shocking! And she four weeks the bride of Baron Illify. Whatever is Egdril thinking of? Form up a guard of honor to escort the good prince." And he waved the young lieutenant to depart on his mission. "Frenery," and when his secretary appeared, "please to let Bishop Wodarick know that his presence is respectfully requested here at the palace for tea. And he is to bring the registry book with him, if he would not mind. We might need that, too." Frenery turned to leave on that errand. "Oh, and tell the chatelaine that Prince Mavron is guesting with us tonight. We'll have to have something more special than the light supper we had ordered."

Consequently when the troop with Mavron at its fore trotted into the courtyard, the prince and princess, flanked by the tall, dignified bishop, welcomed their royal visitor.

"My dear Mavron, how good it is to see you so soon again. What can bring you here?"

"Did not my father leave word that I was to escort the Lady Laurel back to Mauritia?" Mavron's shrewd eyes were watching Princess Willow who regarded him evenly.

"In his note to me, he did say something of the sort but I doubt very much if my sister-in-law will wish to leave."

"Oh, and why?"

"Where are my manners? Do come in, Prince Mavron. Bishop Wodarick has joined us for tea. Surely a cup will do you good after your long ride, and we can forgive your travel dust since we are all informal here,"

"Did you by any chance bring letters from my mother for me, cousin?" Princess Willow asked with a hopeful expression on her face.

Mavron hesitated between one step and another and frowned down.

"But surely you must know, Princess . . ."

"Know what?" Willow's hand went to her chest, her eyes widened with panic.

Jamas thought she had struck just the right tone of surprise in her dissembling.

"That your mother, and indeed, your younger sisters have all left Mauritia?"

"Oh, my, they have?" The princess was the epitome of surprise. "Oh, so they did get permission to visit my paternal uncle in Sarmarland? Mother has wanted to retire there for some time, you know. I believe she asked her majesty's permission for the visit some time ago! That may be why I have not heard. It would take a long time for letters from Sarmarland to arrive here in Esphania, would it not?"

"Sarmarland? Your uncle Barrein?" Mavron absorbed that information and nodded. "Perhaps that is the case, then."

"I'm sure it is," Princess Willow said, teapot pointed over a fresh cup and saucer. "Tea, then? Milk? And no sugar, if I remember correctly."

"Just so."

"Now, about Laurel," Willow said, for she and Jamas had agreed not to prevaricate with Prince Mavron. She smiled and even managed a light giggle. "It was ever so romantic."

"What?" Mavron did not even get a chance for a sip of the tea.

"Why, her elopement."

"Elopement?" Milky tea sloshed over the rim as he precipitously returned the cup to its saucer.

"Yes," and Jamas stretched out his long legs, grinning. "She and my equerry. Baron Grenejon of Illify, you know, my best man. They eloped without a word to anyone. Except the Bishop here who married them."

"You married them without the king's permission?"

Bishop Wodarick had been forewarned and mildly regarded the royal visitor, clasping his hands together so that the ruby bishopric ring flashed in the sun.

"Indeed, my son, I was unaware that permission would be required in the case of Lady Laurel, when she had the permission of her brother-in-law, who, in the absence of the king, could be constituted as her legal guardian."

"Legal guardian?"

"She is of age, as is the baron," the bishop replied gently. "Surely there was no impediment to their union?" he asked, as if the thought had just occurred to him. "She was not married before, was she?"

"Nor even betrothed," said the princess firmly, and she stared back at the prince.

"I . . . I came to escort her back to a wedding: a wedding most felicitously arranged by the queen."

"The queen so enjoys matchmaking, does she not?" Willow said. Then her eyes dropped, following Niffy, who had approached Mavron and was now rubbing herself against his legs. "New boots, cousin?"

Fortunately for the delicate china, Mavron had already deposited cup and saucer on the table beside him because they would surely have slipped from nervous fingers. Mavron went quite pale and then blood suffused his face. His complexion went through several more changes, turning almost purple once. Jamas poured a respectable tot of his best brandy and offered it to his cousin-in-law. Mavron swallowed more than the spirits before he got himself under control again.

Then the Mauritian prince turned to the prelate. "I may have a copy of the marriage certificate?"

"Of course."

"Who witnessed this union?" Mavron gave Jamas and Willow an almost desperate glance.

"We did, of course," she said and left it at that.

Mavron then sighed very deeply and began rubbing his hands on the chamois riding breeches he wore.

"These are, actually, very new boots," he said in the most conversational of tones. "You won't have heard, of course, but my brother Geroge has been laid up the past week with a severe fever. We think he caught cold when he had to ford the River Thuler and did not think to change his wet boots at once."

"Yes, wet boots could be detrimental to one's health," Princess Willow agreed. "But he will recover?"

"Oh yes," Mavron agreed emphatically and his eyes narrowed. "A close call, to be sure, and one can never be too careful, can one?"

"Never," Princess Willow agreed.

"Never," Jamas said, uncrossing his ankles and then reaching down to flick off a small piece of carpet fluff off his own new, highly polished half boots. Mavron watched the action, his face quite thoughtful.

"We trust that the queen remains in good health during this pregnancy?" Willow asked with delicate concern.

Mavron's face was a study in suppressed emotions. "We all hope . . ." and he paused a beat, "that she will soon be delivered of a healthy child."

"A child would be welcome," Willow said, "but a son would be a cause for great rejoicing, would it not? And many new plans."

Mavron rubbed one temple thoughtfully, as if to generate a proper response.

"Do you have the same bootmaker as your father, the king?" Willow asked in the silence.

Mavron fixed his eyes on hers, and she did not break the

contact.

"Would she dare?" was his whispered comment.

"Just wouldn't she!" was Jamas' reply.

Mavron stood then. "I must request an interview with . . ."

"Baroness Laurel," Willow supplied when he looked in her direction for Laurel's new rank. "But, of course. It is high time that pair left their idyll and returned to their duties here at Esphania City."

"I shall send my fastest rider. They can be here by midday tomorrow," Jamas said.

"Come, cousin," Willow said, rising, "let me show you to your quarters while my husband pens the message. I believe you were comfortable in the ones you had on your previous stay with us . . ."

When the door had closed on the two, the bishop leaned toward his prince.

"I had not believed your discreet explanation about the dangers threatening your wife and her sister, but now I do. I mean, *both* the king's sons? Appalling! If there is anything more I can do . . ."

Jamas finished dashing off the few words needed to bring his equerry and bride back to the city and now turned to the bishop.

"No, my lord Bishop, sheltering my inlaws in your summer residence has been a great relief to my wife. Let us hope someone can stop the fiend before she accomplishes whatever it is she wants so badly."

"I would hazard the guess that she is one whom power makes giddy. Only God has the right to dispose life and death, and she has usurped that prerogative." He shook his head sadly. "Power is a very dangerous tool, my son, and some are unsuited to employ it."

"One must be raised to the job," Jamas said.

"Meh!" replied Niffy, settling down again in the sun shining in the windows.

Baron and Baroness Illify arrived just before the bells in the cathedral and town hall indulged in their midday excess. Prince Jamas had taken his cousin-in-law to the registry to inspect the entry for the marriage. Prince Mavron found it in proper order, though he frowned.

"This is the day you and my cousin were married," he said, a finger on the date.

"Yes. You know we all disappeared early. Well, that was why!"

"Oh!"

Then the two men went on a horseback tour of the city, which allowed Jamas to show Prince Mavron all the river defenses. Which were formidable. By the time they returned to the castle, the other newlywed couple were in the morning room, chatting merrily. Willow winked at her husband, which indicated that she had had sufficient time to inform her sister and her husband of all the latest events.

Laurel jumped to her feet when Mavron bowed over her hand and called her "Baroness."

"Oh, I have left you with a disagreeable duty, have I not, Mav. And I wouldn't have done that to you for a million guilders if I'd had any inkling that your father had already arranged a marriage for me."

"Wouldn't you?" Mavron said, raising one dark eyebrow at such guilelessness. But it was patently obvious that the young couple were madly in love with each other. "I suppose I can manage to placate my father. It was more *her* idea." Then he closed his lips on something he had been about to say.

"You will be careful?" Laurel asked.

"You may rest assured on that point," he said, his expression grim. "And on the fact that I have discovered nothing irregular in your elopement, for the bishop has reassured me on that score." Then the prince turned to Jamas. "I think I had best not dally here, and indeed it is with deep regret that I find I should make all haste back to Mauritia."

"You can at least have lunch," Willow said, "to give yourself the energy to return in all speed."

"I accept."

"And," Jamas said earnestly, "should you require the assistance of a friendly neighbor . . ."

Mavron's smile was perfunctory, though the bow he gave Jamas' suggestion was profound. "I shall remember that."

We squeaked out of that one well, didn't we, Niffy?" Jamas said as he and Willow retired to their apartment after bidding Mavron farewell.

"I do hope that Mavron can, too. Unfortunately the queen recognizes an enemy in him . . ."

"And in Geroge, from recent events . . ."

"Geroge was more vocal in trying to persuade his father not to marry again. That woman had no background at all to recommend her to anyone, much less a king."

"Ah, but a king is the very person to raise one in rank, is he not?" Jamas reminded her.

"A king should have twice the ordinary amount of common sense," Willow said, to which Niffy replied with an emphatic "Meeerow!"

"There should be nothing 'common' about a king," Willow added primly.

Jamas tousled the formal curls in which she now wore her beautiful black hair—as befit her new station.

"How much we've learned in the past few weeks!" he teased her.

"Giving myself airs, am I?" Willow said in mock indignation.

"At least, you're not seeing shadows everywhere." The words were no sooner out of his mouth than he regretted them and had to coax her out of the return of her anxiety.

"Are you prescient, my love?" Jamas asked three days later when a courier who had ridden day and night arrived with a missive from Mavron.

"Oh, good heavens, what now?" Willow said. "And it must be important, for here comes Niffy."

"Then it's from Mauritia, isn't it?" put in Laurel who was also at the table with them for lunch. Baron Illify was off on his prince's business.

"Indeed." Jamas frowned at the seal. He had only glanced at the first line when he half rose from his chair in surprise. Niffy let out a wail. "The queen has been delivered prematurely of a son, Geroge has died and the king is now very ill. Mavron requests my presence."

Niffy stretched up, planting her paws on Jamas' thighs and merowing at her most emphatic.

"Yes, yes, Niffy, you'll come, too," Jamas said, stroking the cat's head in reassurance. He passed the letter to his wife. "I'm not at all sure how I can help Mavron, but someone must before that woman takes total control and we discover ourselves dead in our beds from some mysterious ailment."

"What can Niffy do?" Laurel asked, accepting the letter which Willow, looking distraught, handed over to her. "Mavron wrote this himself, too."

"So no one else would know he had sent it." Jamas sat back in his chair, all appetite gone. He locked his fingers together at the back of his head and, tilting his chair, kept his balance by one foot on the substantial leg of the table. "Hmmm." His chair came down with a bang, and he propelled himself out of it, beginning to pace up and down.

Niffy leaped to the chair he had vacated, her almond-shaped eyes watching his progress back and forth. Then he stopped and stared at her.

"All right, Niffy, what *do* we do?"

"How could the cat know?" Laurel asked, laughing a little nervously at her brother-in-law's unexpected whimsy.

Willow raised a finger and waggled at her sister. "Of course, you haven't been around this Niffy-cat as much as I have. Jamas is reasonably certain that the spirit of Mangan somehow inhabits this magnificent—*ooooooh*," and she drew in a long breath of amazement, then burst into laughter. "Of course, how stupid not to have guessed. Magnificat! That's your true name!"

Niffy threw back her head and keened a particularly piercing note and puffed up every hair on her body until she appeared four times her actual size. Laurel recoiled in her chair, but Willow seemed amused.

"Of course it is," Jamas said as he strode back to his chair and cupped Niffy's head in his hand, smiling conspiratorially down at the Magnificat. "How like Mangan. How like Mangan you are, Niffy. Did you think I was so dense as not to add up a few of those equations you were always making me sweat through? Did you think I haven't seen your fine feline hand in much that has happened these last few months? However, you have done it, Mangan-Niffy, you have succeeded in leaving behind an essence to guide me. And I never needed guidance more!"

Niffy's fur gradually subsided to a normal appearance

and, as Jamas' impassioned words died away, she gave a flick of her head and proceeded to groom her shoulders in the satisfied way that cats have when they've won their point— whatever it might be.

Jamas chuckled. "Frenery!" he called. When the good man arrived, he started his instructions. "Send a messenger to retrieve Baron Illify. Ask Moxtell to lend me his sons and his brothers, and I'll want the Fennells, too. Also Prince Temeron, the Duke of Brastock, and ask Bishop Wodarick if I can borrow those two stalwart canons of his . . ."

"Estreger and Memmison?"

"The very ones." As soon as Frenery had hastened off to do his bidding, he turned to Niffy. "Shall we see what books I'm to peruse before I leave, my dear Magniffycat?"

"He means it," Laurel said to her sister.

"Of course he does," Willow replied, blotting her lips. "Go with him and see. I'll pack. Will you need any dress clothes?"

"Funeral attire and something quietly elegant for any formal occasions, but leave room for Niffy," Jamas called over his shoulder as he fiddled with the moulding by the fireplace to gain entrance to the quickest route to Mangan's tower. "Oh," he added, sticking his head around the door, "when Grenejon gets here, send him up."

The door had only just closed behind him when it sprang open again.

"Oh, and you two are coming with us, I think. After all, we must present a solid front, mustn't we? I know your mother can ride, but can Sollie?"

"If we are all going with you, who will guard Esphania?" Willow asked.

"Esphanians!" And this time the door stayed shut.

Sombre banners covered the main gate at Mauritia and informed the hard-riding party that there had been deaths in the royal palace.

"Who goes there?" the captain of the guard demanded, for the gates were also shut.

"The Prince and Princess of Esphania, come to pay respects!"

"I've orders to admit no one. Certainly not an armed company."

"Captain Nesfaru, don't you recognize us?" Willow said, throwing back the hood of her cape. "I'm Lady Willow and here is my sister, Laurel. And Countess Solesne. Surely we may enter and console the grieved."

The captain plainly saw no threat in three women doing what women did best.

"Well, I guess you're all right," he said, grudgingly. "But leave your horses."

"What! Don't be silly, Captain. We can't walk up the hills after travelling as hard as we have," Willow said.

Jamas was delighted to hear his beloved taking charge of events, instead of letting them just happen to her.

"Well . . ." and again he was indecisive.

"We *are* tired and wish to present ourselves to her majesty as soon as possible," Laurel put in.

So he agreed to let them in.

"Jamas, I know I can get orders to admit you, too,"

Countess Solesne murmured to Jamas. "Just dismount and wait."

"Niffy's up behind me now," Willow added as she became aware of a discreet presence under her riding cloak. She tucked the edges in under her legs to provide a safer purchase for the cat. She also felt a lot braver with Niffy entering with them.

A lieutenant and three soldiers escorted them through the silent city—every edifice and most homes showing the black cloth of national mourning—to the palace where even lamp standards were dimmed. Not a word was spoken.

They were taken to the guard post, not the main entrance which was closed by the most enormous, and vulgar, black wreath.

"I thought the captain understood. . . ." the portly officer in charge began as they were announced to him.

"Now, Major Hurell," Countess Solesne said in an admonitory tone, "did you think the princess and baroness would be so lacking in respect for the royal house of Mauritia that they would not hurry to her majesty's side to provide what comfort they could?"

"Oh, I didn't—I mean, I had no idea—"

"We came instantly the news reached us," Willow said, once again taking an initiative.

"Yes, of course you would, your highness," the major said, bowing like a bobbing toy. "It is just the sort of thing you would do." The major had commanded the palace guard the whole time Willow, Laurel, and their mother had been required to live there. "Sad times, indeed, with both the king and Prince Geroge gone. Both in their prime. We've had such bad luck in Mauritia." He shook his head.

"And the new young princeling . . ."

"You refer to his majesty, King Egdril the Second?"

"Of course." Willow took that in her stride and decided not to ask to be shown to Prince Mavron even before she felt claws press against her right side. She had bundled its fold so that no one would be likely to suppose she carried a cat there. "His majesty thrives?"

"Of course," the major said with a sort of huffing of his full cheeks as he nervously stroked his side-whiskers.

"Perhaps we should go directly to the Duchess Insaphar, Salinah? Is she here?"

"Where else would she be?"

No one challenged that, especially since the major now gave orders for them to be escorted to the palace.

Inside, the palace was colder than a morgue and darker. Not a painting, portrait, or *objet d'art* but wasn't draped in sable. Their footsteps echoed through corridors, totally devoid of petitioners and minor officials.

"She can't have killed them all off?" Laurel murmured to her sister.

"Silence, please," the young and officious lieutenant whispered over his shoulder at them.

They went through the public rooms and up the long flight of stairs that branched at the top. A row of guards stood across the right hand turning which would lead into the royal quarters. So they took the left-hand side where only two men stood sentinel. They immediately crossed their shrouded pike heads to prevent entry.

"Who goes there?"

"Lieutenant of the Palace Guard and three female visitors."

"The Princess of Esphania, the Baroness Illify, and the Countess Solesne," the countess said in a low but intense voice, designed to make the callow quiver. "To see Baroness Salinah."

"Wait here," said one of the flunkies.

"We will not," the countess said and, flipping up the pikes, walked determinedly down the hall, her two former charges following as purposefully.

"I say, there, you can't do that . . ." the lieutenant called after them.

"We can and we have," muttered the countess, flouncing her riding skirt as she lengthened her stride.

Their footsteps echoed in the halls and, when they passed the first door, they were conscious of its being opened a crack and then closed.

"Has she got everyone kennelled up like so many disobedient children?" Willow murmured, appalled that a once bustling palace was reduced to the silence of the crypt.

"And where is Mavron? He should ascend the throne, not a baby," said Laurel.

"Nonsense, how else can that woman gain complete control unless she gets herself appointed as regent for her son."

A muted "MeOW!" issued from Willow's bundled cloak.

"Yes, I know, Niffy," the princess said and patted it reassuringly. "She'll give the word 'regent' a bad smell."

FINALLY they arrived at the entrance to Salinah's apartment. It was not guarded, so Willow tapped at the door. When there was no answer, she rapped a little more loudly. Pressing her ear against the door, she listened.

"There's someone in there," she murmured.

"Then, we shall enter," the countess said and, turning the handle, pulled open the door. And stopped.

"Oh, for heaven's sake." For a barrier of furniture filled the doorway. "Salinah! It's Countess Solesne. I've come to rescue you."

"From what are we rescuing her?" Willow asked in surprise.

"Well, it must be something. I can't really imagine a girl of Salinah's nature piling all that up unless she's scared out of her knickers!"

"Who's there?" a tremulous voice demanded.

"Sollie, with Willow and Laurel," the countess said and began to dismantle the barricade.

"Willow and Laurel? Oh, my God, they must go immediately. They're no more safe here than I am," but the visitors could hear chairs and tables being moved.

Shortly there was a narrow lane free enough for them to squeeze through.

"Close that door," cried Salinah, sounding more like herself.

"Why don't you lock it?" Laurel asked but discovered

there was no key just as Salinah remarked acidly that no one could lock a door in Castle Mauritia anymore. "And you're the cause of that!" she said when the three emerged into clearer space.

"And how do you arrive at that conclusion?" Willow asked, surprised. Though she hadn't thought that anything Salinah said or did could surprise her.

"Locked doors mean subversive activities, of course."

"And all that pile of furniture isn't a subversive obstruction."

"Why are you here? You won't get out now you've got in, you know, and why you came back, I cannot imagine," said Salinah in her usual manner and then ruined the impression by bursting into tears and collapsing against Willow. "But I'm so glad to see you."

They got the now hysterical girl calmed down sufficiently to learn why she was barricading herself in her room as best she could.

"Yasmin's betrothed me to that puling baby!" Salinah was indignant. "She's put Mavron in jail and is beheading him in the morning." She wept a little more. "She had filled Egdril's room with all her little minions. The moment the king expired, she had the prince seized. But he couldn't not be at his father's deathbed, could he? And his men were outnumbered, especially when all *her* guards swarmed in on top of them. Not even Mavron thought she would move that fast. I warned him, but he wouldn't listen to me. Even when I *told* him that *she'd* planned for him to be dead, too, before she finished Egdril off. So what can you possibly do about it?"

"There's only one thing we can do about it," Willow said, removing her cloak and releasing Niffy.

Salinah sprang to her feet, jumping back and away from the cat, both hands outstretched in a defensive position.

"You brought that cat?" Her eyes, already dark from weeping and frustration, widened even more at the sight of Niffy shaking her ruffled fur into place. "Are you mad? The queen'll skewer it the moment she sees it."

"Ah, but she won't see it, will she, Salinah?" Willow said. "And the only thing we can do about Yasmin is get rid of her, and that solves the entire problem. Doesn't it?"

"And how under the twin suns and the triple moons could you possibly do that?" Salinah's haughty pose once more dissolved into tears. "But that is the only solution, isn't it?"

"There now," the countess said, holding the once overly proud baroness in a motherly embrace. "You've been very brave, my dear." Willow and Laurel exchanged surprised glances but decided that Sollie was taking the right tack. "And in such a terrible state. You don't look as if you've eaten . . . or bathed in days."

"I haven't," sobbed Salinah. "One doesn't dare. She might be ready to poison me next. And I had to act charmed and pleased that she wanted me to marry that . . . that awful child of hers. You should see it!" Her face contorted in disgust. "I don't even think it's human! It can't be the king's! You didn't bring something to eat, did you?" she asked piteously.

Laurel reached into her travel pouch and brought out some bread and cheese, which Salinah grabbed from her hands and devoured, tearing off pieces and stuffing them into her mouth.

Niffy was now quartering the room, once such a graceful setting for the red-haired duchess. She paused by the fireplace and meowed.

"Sometimes people have no imagination," Willow said as

she went to Niffy's assistance.

"Well, chimney breasts can supply sufficient room, you know," the countess said. "And I do know that there's a warren between the walls of this place. Niffy, will you be all right on your own? It's a long way over to the royal wing. Shouldn't you wait for the prince?"

Niffy twitched her tail expressively.

"I don't think Jamas is included in her plans," Willow said, feeling along the ornate moulding for a loose section. "Ah," and she twisted the portion. Slowly a panel beside her swung open.

"Not the fireplace," Laurel said.

Willow looked inside. "Dark."

"That's where Niffy's invaluable," Laurel said.

"Good luck, dear," Willow said as the cat, tail tip idly moving, made her way into the hidden passage. "And don't get hurt!" she added. She did not quite close the panel. "Just in case we don't hear her when she returns. That's a thick panel."

"Didn't you think to store up any provisions for yourself?" Sollie asked Salinah, who was slumped in the corner of the one couch still available to be used for its original function.

"Of course, but they're all gone."

"Surely she's not starving all the people . . ." the countess began.

"I can't trust anyone," Salinah said sullenly, finding a stray crumb in her lap. She wet a fingertip and transferred it to her mouth.

"She can't have poisoned the water . . ." The countess indicated Salinah's gown which looked as if the girl had not changed it in days.

"I wouldn't put it past her," came from Salinah.

"Isn't it fortunate I came prepared, then," the countess said and, reaching into her own travel pouch, drew out several items.

"More food?"

"No. Antidotes, and litmus papers which will detect the acid of poison."

"A lot of good that does when I have nothing left to test it on."

"Surely you can ring for service . . ."

"And have them discover you all here?" Salinah widened her eyes in contempt for that suggestion.

"When guards escorted us up?" the countess demanded.

"Ohhhhh," and Salinah actually wailed like a frightened child.

"Well, I am not going any longer without some refreshment," the countess said and, before Salinah could stop her, went to the bellpull and gave it several yanks.

"They'll never answer," Salinah moaned.

A moment later the pneumatic speaking tube whistled a response.

Countess Solesne went to it, opening the cover, and in the clear loud voice needed for orders to reach the subterranean pantries, she announced that the Baroness Salinah required hot water for tea and refreshments for four. "Generous portions," she added.

"They'll never come."

They did, for the dumbwaiter bell rang not five minutes later and, when Willow opened the hatch, they could all hear the squeaking of the platform being hoisted to their level.

"Well, I hope the cook could spare it," the countess said as she looked at what had been laid out for their consumption.

"She is carrying mourning a trifle too far. Especially since she contrived to have so many funerals."

Salinah hauled the countess away from the hatch as if the words would have carried through the thick wood and down to the pantry.

"Nonsense, Salinah. Get a hold of yourself. You're the courageous young woman who hunted barguas and boar. What's happened to you? And thank heavens, the water is hot enough to make a respectable cup."

"But you don't dare . . ."

The countess snorted but took several of her papers out of the packet and tested them against the bread and butter—and not much butter—against the dry Madeira slices, and everything on the tray.

"It's all safe enough to eat." And she proceeded to do so, making the tea as well and passing the plates round.

Willow and Laurel ate sparingly to allow Salinah to make up for lost meals, but the countess ate what was a fair share. Only when Salinah reached for the milk pitcher to pour the remainder in her cup did the countess stay her hand.

"Niffy will be thirsty when she returns from those dusty passageways."

Salinah paused, her face reflecting skepticism as well as indignation. "What makes you so sure the cat will come back? Or get back."

"As you saw at Vial Woods, she's a self-reliant personage and a formidable hunter," Willow said. Then, making a bed of discarded cushions and pillows, she settled herself down for a rest. "I suggest you all follow my example. We might need to be rested for whatever else we have to do today."

Salinah gave a contemptuous sniff, but the meal had obviously restored her spirits. "Could I have one of those papers of yours, Sollie? I really would like to have a quick bath . . . if the water's safe."

"Of course, my dear," and Sollie handed one over. Then she followed Willow's example, as did Laurel, while Salinah indulged herself.

Willow did not sleep although she closed her eyes. She kept wondering what Jamas was doing and if he'd heard about Mavron. She could almost imagine the scene in Egdril's bedchamber, with Mavron in filial attendance and doubtless, that woman, exuding solicitousness for her dying husband, just waiting until he had been pronounced dead before she entrapped the true heir to the throne. And what was Niffy doing now? Even a long-legged clever cat person would require a long time to reach the royal apartments and penetrate rooms which were most assuredly well guarded. And what did Niffy plan to do once she had entered that woman's rooms? Or, more to the point, what did Mangan hope to achieve by such a surreptitious entry?

In spite of her worrisome thoughts, Willow did fall asleep. So did the other three women.

What awakened her was something delicately nibbling her ear.

"Niffy?" Willow hugged the cat to her in an excess of relief. Another noise made her sit bolt upright, for through the wide-open panel came the dark shadows of large figures.

"Ssst, Willow, it's me!" Jamas' unmistakable whisper reassured her. Though what she could have done to prevent deadly intruders, Willow didn't know.

"How did you find Niffy?"

"Oh, she found us," Jamas said, hunkering down by his wife and running a loving finger along her face. "You're all right?"

"Jamas, you must save Mavron. She's going to behead him tomorrow."

"Said and done," Jamas said with a low laugh.

That was enough to waken Salinah, who sat up, saw all the dark figures, and opened her mouth to scream. The man nearest her clapped a hand across her mouth and nearly lost his grip when she bit him and kicked out savagely. But he had the advantage of position.

"Easy, Salinah," Jamas said, "it's one of Moxtell's lads. He won't harm you, but we really don't need to broadcast our arrival, now do we? Mavron, reassure the duchess,"

"I'll light some candles, shall I?" Laurel said, rising and doing so. "Phewww, what is that smell?" she asked, sniffing.

"I suspect it is me," Mavron said.

"Oh, your poor hands," Salinah said, reaching for them so that all saw the cruel marks manacles had gouged in his wrists. "You come with me. She hasn't poisoned the water, and I've some salve that will ease these immediately."

The others watched as Salinah led Mavron off to minister to him.

"*How* did Niffy find you? Where did she find you?"

Jamas chuckled as he settled down on the couch, pulling Willow beside him. "Rather a long story, and the night is not over yet. I'm happy to say that there are many Mauritians who are not pleased with the recent events. And were delighted to find someone who might adjust matters.

"We found the postern gate and also some interesting comings and goings." He chuckled. "So we joined forces with those determined to restore the throne to its rightful claimant. They knew all the back ways and, since we had a superior force, we overwhelmed the dungeon guards and released

Mavron. We got as far as the kitchens—here we also discovered more like minded folk—when who bursts upon the scene but Niffy here."

"What was she doing in the kitchens?" Willow said, bending an accusatory stare on the cat, who was vigorously washing her dirty paws.

"Hungry, I imagine. We were," Jamas said, flipping open his cape on the floor and displaying a variety of foods, including a whole roasted fowl, breads, fruits, cheeses, and a flagon of wine.

"All we got was dry bread and cake," Willow said, reaching first for the flagon to wet her throat while Jamas neatly severed a leg from the fowl and handed it to her. "Oh, this is good," she muttered around the drumstick. She offered a sliver to Niffy. The cat was prowling back and forth from Jamas to the still-open panel.

"I think she wants us to move now," Jamas said with a sigh and rose. Willow did, too. He tried to push her back down.

"I'm coming with you!"

Jamas held up his hands defensively at her purposeful tone. "If you insist."

"I do," she said and stripped off her riding skirt since she could move more easily in the britches she wore underneath.

"I'm not waiting around again, either," Laurel said, doing the same thing.

"I think I will," the countess said, reaching for another piece of cheese. "I'm not at my best anymore crawling around dark and dusty places."

"What dark and dusty places?" Salinah demanded, returning with Mavron, whose wrists were now bandaged neatly. He was also wearing fresh clothing of an informal nature, though how Salinah had managed to fit him from what was generally in a woman's wardrobe remained a bit of a mystery. At least to everyone but Mavron.

"Just before dawn is the very best time to catch your enemy out," Jamas said, shifting his sword on his hip.

"Who?" demanded Salinah.

"Her, of course," Mavron said. "With any luck, she's asleep and dreaming happily of seeing my head bounce down the palace steps."

"Ohhh, ugh!" Salinah gave a massive shudder. "How can you jest about it?"

"Easily enough," Mavron said, "since now it won't happen, thanks to Jamas and my loyal subjects."

There was a rumble of deep voices "here-here-ing, your majesty," but softly. As most of the men had darkened their faces with soot, Willow couldn't tell who was who, Esphanian or Mauritian. She did identify the Moxtell sons and brothers by height and bulk. She thought she recognized one or two Mauritians— soldiers from the household guards.

Niffy said an imperious "MaaaaROW!"

"Coming," Jamas said, grinning all around, and he obediently followed the purposeful cat into the passageway.

Some of the cobwebs had been stirred by recent usage, and they heard the scurryings of frightened small creatures, but these did not cause anyone a moment's concern. Traversing such dark ways, however, with only the flickering of torches and candles did make the journey seem endless.

When the forward movement stopped, it was so abrupt that Willow ran into Jamas. He'd nearly stepped on Niffy. There were low exclamations of surprise from behind them.

Then Jamas saw a little spot of light at eye level and

realized that they had reached Niffy's destination. Putting his eye to the hole, he peeked once and drew back.

Turning to Willow, he whispered right into her ear.

"We're in *her* bedchamber and she is asleep."

Willow made a strangled sound, pointing to the floor as Niffy pushed open a panel and disappeared . . . into the chamber. The panel began to shut silently behind her.

"Huh?" Jamas whirled round to see the tip of Niffy's tail disappearing. "Whoa . . ." He cut off the sound he had inadvertently made by clapping his hand to his mouth. He peered anxiously back through the spy-hole to be sure he hadn't been heard inside the room. He gave a single nod of his head in relief.

Mavron tapped Willow's shoulder, and she could just make out the querying look on his face. So she passed him word of what had just happened. Just then, Jamas gestured for Willow to peek through the hole. He was grinning broadly.

If Willow had not known that Niffy was in the room, she might have just thought—as the drowsing guards about the royal bed would have, had they been as alert as they should have been—that a shadow moved stealthily around the room and to the bed, centered on the longest wall. Willow wondered if Mangan had chosen Niffy especially for her dark fur, so suitable for lurking in dark corners. Then she remembered Jamas saying that Mangan told him Niffy had done the choosing.

Willow was conscious of a noise, an odd one: a soft snore in fact. And since the guards were all standing, more or less, the noise emanated from the bed. Her eyes adjusting to the dim light, Willow now realized that the queen lay on her back, arms outstretched, her mouth slightly ajar. How very unattractive, she thought.

A touch on her shoulder and she gave way to Mavron, who breathed out a noise of satisfaction, Willow thought, or maybe contempt. Several others, including Salinah, took their turn at the peek hole, squeezing past each other in the tight passage. Then Laurel hssted at Jamas to come quickly to see.

Jamas took a quick look, then pulled Willow to the hole, and she gave way to Mavron.

Niffy had reached the head of the bed, climbing silently up the hangings, until she could step onto the surface, still in shadow. Willow saw her creeping slowly, with delicate stalking steps across the pillows to the sleeper's head.

"What is she planning to do?" Willow mouthed to Jamas who shrugged as he put his lips to her ear to answer.

"She usually knows what she's doing, even if we don't."

Careful shufflings and those in the vanguard had a chance to look in on the bedchamber. The oldest Moxtell son asked why they were waiting. Jamas could only shrug. They were beginning to notice that the air in the secret passageway was becoming fusty with all of them in a space where there was little ventilation.

"She's curling herself up on the pillow now," Willow said, for it was her eye occupying the peephole. "Right beside her head!"

Jamas crowded in and almost instantly a sharp noise could be heard. He drew back his head so his eye would not be noticed.

"Ooops," he said noncommittally.

"What?" Mavron mouthed.

"She sneezed."

"Who? The cat?"

"The queen," Jamas murmured. He peeped in again. Then all of them heard an outraged cry. "Niffy scratched her cheek!"

"Is Niffy all right?" Willow asked anxiously.

"She just scrambled up the bed curtains and out of sight."

The sneezing continued, punctuated by irate screams and imprecations until the sneezing became so constant the queen couldn't do anything else. She now sat bolt upright in bed, eyes watering, one hand on her cheek, trying to give orders to guards on the expiration of each sneeze.

"The reason she hates cats," Salinah murmured with a malicious grin, "is because she's so violently allergic to them!"

From the bedchamber the covert watchers heard her rantings.

"Find that . . . (sneeze) . . . cat. (sneeze) It scrat(sneeze)ched me. Find . . . (sneeze) it! *Now!* Who (sneeze, sneeze) let (sneeze, gasp) the (gasp sneeze sneeze) mon(sneeze)ster in? I'll . . . (sneeze, gasp, choke, sniff) chop off his (sneeze)—!"

The queen had bounced out of her bed, sneezing, each new explosion more forceful so that she could barely stand upright. She clung to the bedpost, gasping for breath in between monumental sneezes.

"FIND IT!"

The guards were running here and there trying to locate a cat. No one thought of the bed drapes—and the queen had been too paralyzed by her sneezing to have heard Niffy's rapid ascent. The guards looked behind the curtains at the windows, under the furniture, in the wardrobes, while the queen became more and more helpless with her paroxysm.

Jamas took a good look at the woman who had caused so much trouble. She was small, even swathed by the voluminous nightdress, and not even remotely appealing. His Willow gave a polite little whisper of a sneeze on the one occasion he had heard her. Not these great gusty violent affairs. Queen Yasmin's face, contorted by the sneezing and the one cheek marked by a single thin claw line, was pinched and her features more sharp than classic. Perhaps in full court regalia and her charms artfully enhanced cosmetically, she might have been more attractive. Certainly the tangled mess of teased hair that framed her face added nothing to her appearance. Jamas did wonder how she had contrived to dominate Egdril for eight years or longer. She might just have been prettier when she was younger. She certainly was not pretty now, sneezing, snorting, her nose running, screaming when she had the breath for it—for her maid, for her physician, for help.

All of a sudden her body went rigid and her face froze into a mask of horror. She clutched once at her chest and then fell to the floor, eyes staring—almost accusingly, Jamas thought—in his direction.

"She's dead, I think."

The guards waited only long enough to come to the same conclusion before they bolted out the door, yelling at the top of their lungs. Jamas didn't know if they screamed from relief, for salvation, or just for someone in authority to come and take over.

"Now, where is the release mechanism?" he asked as Mavron reached across him and pressed something.

A section of the wall swung open.

"Niffy?" Jamas called, concerned until her face appeared over the top of the bed hangings.

"Meh!" she said with great satisfaction and, reversing her body, lowered herself, tail first, by clever claws to the point where she could make an easy leap to the floor without bruising her paw pads.

"Such a good cat! Such a clever cat!" Jamas tried to take her up in his arms but she eluded him. She made for the washstand and looked imperiously over her shoulder at him.

"She needs to wash her paws, I suspect," Willow said and hastened to pour water in the over-decorated and gilded porcelain basin.

Neatly Niffy jumped up to the stand and then into the water, where she walked around and around, her claws scraping the china. Just then Mavron and the Moxtell sons and brothers, filing into the bedchamber, exclaimed in surprise at seeing a cat deliberately immersing itself.

"She's always played with water," Jamas said, half-amused and half-annoyed at their reaction.

Willow found a clean towel and spread it on the floor for Niffy to dry her feet on. Niffy spent a good time in the water until she was satisfied that she had rinsed off whatever it was she had put on her claws.

With a face devoid of expression, Mavron stripped the embroidered satin cover from the bed and flipped it negligently over the corpse of his stepmother. Then he brushed his hands together, straightened his shoulders and turned to the assembled, every inch the royal personage he was.

"As my first official duty as King of Mauritia, let me thank my loyal allies and subjects for their assistance throughout this . . . ah . . ."

"Regrettable hiatus?" Jamas suggested, grinning.

"Long live King Mavron!" one of the Mauritians said in a loud and penetrating voice.

"Long live King Mavron!" Salinah echoed as they all heard a commotion in the hall.

The group that paused on the threshold just stared, some briefly, before they turned to flee down the hall as fast as their legs could carry them. Others remained, relief showing in their pale faces as they turned with hopeful expressions to Mavron.

It took the rest of the morning to restore order to the palace and city. Mavron evidently had had time to consider the most necessary steps to be taken. Firmly ushering everyone out of the death chamber, he led all to his own apartments. There, installed in his office, he barked out orders, wrote more, called for messengers, and generally organized the start of his reign.

By dinnertime, elation had dissolved into fatigue, and it was a weary group who joined Mavron for an informal meal. King Mavron installed Niffy on her own chair with a table just the right height for her to eat from a dish of livers and other tender morsels which he himself had interviewed the chef to provide.

"I never thought I'd be so grateful to a cat," he told Jamas and Willow with a fond smile at Niffy. The effects of his incarceration were still etched on his face. He had chosen a coat with sufficient lace on the cuff to cover the bandages. "However did you train her to do such things, Jamas? She was magnificent."

"Mrraow?" Niffy looked up from her plate, her almond-shaped green eyes wide.

Jamas cleared his throat hastily, lest Mavron inadvertently speak her private name.

"Actually, she's extremely intelligent and not just for a cat."

"Meh!" Niffy said.

"Special breeding, you see," Jamas went on in the most indolent tone, turning his wineglass and leaving red semicircles on the white table linen. "My regent bred her. And trained her, for that matter." He cleared his throat again. "She's been a great help to me, I can assure you. Warning me now and then, and always to my advantage."

"Ah, yes," Mavron said, indulgently, "forewarned is forearmed, isn't it."

"Meh!"

As it was then, so it is now!